DAISY'S SEARCH FOR ANSWERS

THE EYMANN FAMILY TRILOGY – BOOK 2
AN AMISH ROMANCE

Naomi Troyer

Contents

Chapter 1
Strawberry Baby

"We'll be back in a few hours, Daisy. Do you need anything from town?" Celia called from the front door on her way out.

Daisy smiled at her sister and shook her head. "Nee, denke. Good luck."

Daisy Eymann couldn't help but be grateful that it wasn't her heading into town. It was spring break for the small Amish schoolhouse, where Daisy was a teacher's assistant, and right now she was just enjoying her holiday.

Besides, it wasn't as if her older sister Celia was going to do the weekly marketing. She was going to get everything she needed for tomorrow's celebration. Celia had been cooking and baking since the day before to make sure that every guest would have more than enough to feast on after their brother's wedding.

Daisy still couldn't imagine her brother, Lucas, being a husband. After so many years of not even bothering to go to Sunday singings, Daisy had just come to accept that her brother would probably never get married. But from the very first moment he and Sarah Hauptfleisch had connected, it had been love at first sight.

It was still hard for Daisy to accept the events that had led her brother and Sarah to fall in love. Just like it was still hard for her to accept what her brother had discovered.

She let out a heavy sigh as she brewed a fresh pot of tea. Her mother, Lydia Eymann, would wake up from her afternoon nap shortly. Before she did, Daisy needed to put the demons that haunted her mind to rest.

With her mother suffering from Alzheimer's, a very progressive type, Daisy knew that every second she spent with her mother had to be cherished.

Even if she had so many questions about what Lucas had learned six months before.

Daisy had always just accepted that her copper red hair had been inherited from a distant relative in a long line of Eymanns. Never in a million years would she have guessed that she was adopted.

When her brother had revealed the news to both her and her sister, Daisy had been dumbstruck for the first few weeks. It had been as if she had been living in a world she didn't recognize.

She kept thinking someone was going to tell her it was just a dream.

But six months later, she was still stuck in that very same dream.

Only now, it had become a nightmare.

Daisy couldn't remember the last time she had enjoyed a night of restful sleep. Instead, every evening her dreams were haunted by images of red-haired women and strange men who kept calling her theirs. It was disturbing, to say the least.

But worse than disturbing was the fact that it had a woken a strange curiosity in Daisy about her birth parents. She didn't blame Lydia and Noah for adopting her, she didn't even blame them for keeping it a secret. She was grateful to them for the life and the family they had given her.

But what Daisy did struggle with was why her real parents had given her away. Didn't they want her? Didn't they love her?

Why would they bring a blessing from Gott into this world only to give it away?

The pot of tea whistled on the wood stove, bringing Daisy back to the present. Now wasn't the time to focus on her adoption, or how it haunted her. It was time to wake her mother.

She poured two cups of tea and set them in the living room before she went to rouse her mother.

For a moment Daisy stood in the door and just watched her mother lay sleeping on the bed. Daisy couldn't help but wonder if it was just her imagination, but it seemed her mother was shrinking in size even as her mind faded away.

Her mother was thin, her once full cheeks hollow. Her eyes, that had always sparkled with affection and acceptance, now often were nothing but distant and lost.

Daisy's heart clenched in her chest. She couldn't imagine a worse fate than watching your mother slowly fading away as Alzheimer's stole her memory bit by bit.

"Mamm," she whispered, moving towards the bed. "It's time for you to wake up."

Lydia Eymann stirred with a smile curving her mouth. "There she is, my strawberry boppli."

Daisy smiled at the pet name. Ever since she could remember, her mother had called her that. *My strawberry baby.* Daisy knew they attributed it to the color of her hair.

Hair she didn't inherit from Lydia.

"Kumm, let's go have tea," Daisy coaxed her mother out of bed.

She settled her mother in her favorite seat by the window in the living room before handing her the cup of tea. "I can't believe Lucas is getting married tomorrow."

Lydia's eyes widened with joyful surprise. "Lucas, my Lucas? Ach, what wunderbaar news!"

Daisy smiled, although it made her heart ache to do so. Over the last two months, they had told Lydia the news repeatedly, but as with most of her other memories, she seemed to forget almost as soon as they informed her of the happy news.

"Jah, Sarah is moving in tomorrow. That means tonight you'll be sleeping in your new room. Do you remember you're moving to Lucas's room?" Daisy asked gently.

They had agreed that Lucas and his new bride were to share the main bedroom, while their mother moved to Lucas's room.

Lydia had insisted on this herself in a clear moment, but Daisy wanted to make sure she didn't forget.

"I think so. You moved my things already, didn't you?" her mother asked with an uncertain frown.

"That's right," Daisy smiled, relieved. "We moved most of your things yesterday."

"Jah, I remember that." Lydia took a sip of her tea and turned to Daisy with a confused expression. "I'm sorry. Have we met?"

It was all Daisy could do not to burst out in tears. She smiled and gave her mother a moment alone while she went to hide in the kitchen. How was it possible that Celia could go on and pretend as if nothing had changed since learning about their adoptions?

How was it that Lucas could focus on his wedding without even trying to learn why his parents didn't want him?

Was it wrong for Daisy to want to learn more about her birth parents now that she knew she was adopted? Especially since the woman she had known to be her mother her entire life was having a hard time remembering her name these days?

She felt guilty for wanting to learn more about her past, but she felt as if she wouldn't come to terms with it if she didn't.

Daisy shoved the overwhelming feelings aside, vowing that after the wedding there would be plenty of time to revisit them. But for now, she had to focus on Lucas and Sarah's big day.

Chapter 2
A Celery Celebration

On the day of Lucas's wedding, the entire Eymann household was up at dawn. As Lucas was marrying the bishop's daughter, it was tradition to be held at the home of the bride.

It was a mad rush as chores were in haste, after which they loaded two buggies with all the food and desserts Celia had baked over the last few days. By eight o'clock, Daisy, along with her sister, her brother, and her mother arrived at the home of Bishop Hauptfleisch.

The ceremony was to start at ten o'clock, which meant that tables had to be set out, refreshment tables needed to be stationed outside, and the decorations in the barn needed to be done before the guests arrived.

As Daisy worked tirelessly while the Bishop's wife looked after her mother, she noticed how many people had come to witness her brother's wedding. She had seen Sunday services which were bigger than most, and even a wedding or two that had more people than she'd ever seen at once.

But she had never seen so many people as the group that were waiting in the barn by the time the ceremony had to start.

Lucas and Sarah had chosen both Celia and Daisy as newehockers for the bride. As attendants of the bride, they wore the same color dress as the bride, and would sit in the front of the ceremony.

The ceremony was long, almost tirelessly so for Daisy. After two hours of preaching and singing hymns, the bishop finally called in Lucas and Sarah, who had been privately counseled by a deacon the entire time.

Daisy's eyes burned with tears when her brother stood in front of the congregation. From today, he would no longer just be her big brother, he would become a husband as well.

His clean-shaven jaw would soon boast a beard and it would soon divide his attention between the farm and his wife.

The bishop smiled at Sarah before he asked Lucas the first vow. "Do you promise that if something ever afflicted Sarah with a bodily weakness, sickness, or some other circumstance, that you will care for her as if fitting a Christian husband?"

Lucas nodded solemnly. "I solemnly promise."

The bishop repeated the question for Sarah before he turned to Lucas to ask the second vow. "Do you solemnly promise with one another that you will love and bear and be patient with each other and shall not separate from each other until Gott shall part you from each other through death?"

Both Lucas and Sarah's clear *jah* could be heard throughout the barn where the ceremony was being held.

The bishop smiled, satisfied. "Then I pronounce you mann and frau."

Loud cheers rung through the barn, as celery stalks stood on every available surface. Daisy still didn't know their importance, only that they had been growing celery in excess ever since Lucas announced his wedding day.

The congregation and guests took turns congratulating the bride and groom, while Daisy snuck away to check on her mother. Blissfully unaware of the significance of today, her mother sat on the bishop's porch rocking back and forth.

"Mamm, Lucas is officially a married mann." Daisy announced with a beaming smile as she joined her mother on the porch.

Lydia turned to her with a frown. "Lucas? Do we know him?"

Daisy sighed with disappointment. When Celia had told her it would be best for her mother to stay on the porch because she was a little confused, Daisy had thought her sister was being overly cautious.

Now she understood her mother was having a bad day.

"It's all right Mamm, you can meet him later. Do you need anything?" Daisy asked, longing for the days her mother had looked at her with affection and recognition in her gaze.

"Nee, nee. I'm just waiting for Noah. He's probably in a hurry to get home," Lydia said with a calm smile.

Daisy knew she shouldn't argue. She knew her mother's condition wasn't any fault of her own, but just now and then; like on days like today,she wished she could shake her mother until she remembered.

She bit back the tears that stung her eyes and joined the celebration inside the house. She wasn't hungry. Her appetite had vanished with her mother's memory, but it would be rude not to indulge in creamed celery and stuffed celery chicken.

If she ate anything, she had to at least eat the traditional wedding dishes.

It took her almost thirty minutes to serve herself a plate before she found a quiet spot on the back porch to eat. Her heart was heavy, although it was the happiest day of her brother's life.

Daisy couldn't help but feel as if her world was falling apart a little more every day since learning about her adoption. First, her mother's memory was failing, now Lucas had a new family…

How long before she didn't matter to them at all?

Just like she hadn't mattered to her real parents.

"Daisy, there you are. I've been searching for you everywhere." Celia's voice brought Daisy back to the moment.

Daisy smiled sadly up at her sister. "I just needed a minute…"

"Are you all right?" Celia asked, sitting down beside her. "You know you can confide in me."

Daisy shook her head. Her rampant thoughts had already ruined the day for her. She wouldn't let them ruin Celia's day as well. "I'll be fine. Lucas looks happy, doesn't he?"

Celia nodded with a smile. "Happier than I've ever seen him before."

"For today, that's all that matters. Go on, I'll be back in a minute." Daisy encouraged.

Celia searched her eyes for a moment before she nodded. "All right, but promise you'll talk to me if something is wrong?"

Daisy nodded, but deep down she knew she couldn't tell Celia how she felt. Her sister would wave her feelings away and tell her she was being foolish.

But how could it be foolish to feel as if you're losing the only family you know and to never have known the family where you belong?

Chapter 3
Everyone is Moving On

Sarah moved in with them two days after the wedding. Daisy hadn't been sure what to expect from having another woman in the house, but Sarah had proved to be nothing but kind and considerate.

Which was a great feat, considering she was the new lady of the house. Daisy had feared that Sarah would want to change their routines and interfere with dinner arrangements.

Since she worked at the social services offices in town three days a week, she was happy for Celia and Daisy to continue as they had been doing things over the last few years.

Sarah offered to help with the dishes every night, and with no one asking her to, she had taken to spending time with Lydia in the evenings after dinner. One would've thought she'd rather spend time with Lucas, but Sarah read the bible to Lydia every evening before she retired with Lucas for the night.

It was hard not to like her new sister-in-law when she was as close to perfect as they came. Daisy was grateful for Sarah bringing Lucas joy, but she hoped Sarah could help her as well.

Not that she didn't want to talk to Celia about what was bothering her; it was just a matter of hoping that Sarah would understand her feelings better.

Although the nightmares kept interrupting her sleep, Daisy continued to pretend that nothing was wrong. She bided her time until two weeks after the wedding before she got Sarah alone.

Celia had gone to do the week's marketing in town, and Lucas was working in the fields. Her mother had just laid down for her afternoon nap, which meant that they wouldn't be interrupted for at least a couple of hours.

Daisy's heart raced as she walked into the kitchen to find Sarah sitting at the table.

"Would you like some tea?" Daisy offered with a hopeful smile.

"That would be wunderbaar, denke." Sarah looked up with a smile. "I was just reading about ways to entice shy kinner to play in group games."

"You enjoy working at the kindergarten center, don't you?" Daisy returned to the table with two cups of tea.

"Jah, very much. It saddens my heart to think that those kinner have no one but their foster parents. At least for a few hours a day I like to make them feel like they belong… like they're wanted and not just off casts of parents that didn't care." Sarah let out a sigh. "I'm sorry. I didn't mean to sound negative. What social services are doing for those kinner is wunderbaar, I just wish we could do more."

Daisy nodded. Until six months ago, she hadn't even known she was adopted. She had a carefree childhood filled with love and affection.

She couldn't imagine being a child with no one in the world, knowing that your home was temporary. "You're a kind woman to care for them."

"Denke." Sarah smiled. "How are you doing? You've kept very much to yourself as of late. You used to talk all the time… is it because of me? Are you uncomfortable having me around?"

Daisy could kick herself for giving Sarah that impression. "Nee, nee, not at all. Actually…." Daisy drew in a deep breath and gathered her courage. "Actually, I've had a lot on my mind."

"Would you like to tell me about it?" Sarah asked kindly.

Daisy nodded. Once again, the tears that kept threatening to fall burned her eyes. She had held them back since learning about the adoption and refused to let them fall. How could she regret the life she had when there were children that never had a family adopt them at all?

"I feel foolish for saying this out loud, but I… I'm having trouble accepting the fact that I was adopted. Not that I regret being raised by my parents, Lydia and Noah, but more feeling abandoned by my actual parents. I just feel…"

Sarah reached for her hand and offered her an encouraging smile. "Your feelings are never wrong. They're yours. So don't fear expressing them."

Daisy nodded and swallowed past the lump in her throat. "Everything is just changing so fast. Lucas has you; Celia has Mamm, and I have no one."

"You still have Lucas and Celia and your mamm and me being here doesn't change that."

"I know, but in a way, it does. And there's nothing wrong with that," Daisy quickly added. "It just feels like Celia and Lucas aren't even bothered about being adopted. But with Lucas getting married and Mamm fading away a little more every day… I just wonder about my actual parents."

Sarah nodded with understanding in her gaze. "It's normal to wonder about them. I don't think any adopted child hasn't."

"I have these dreams… dreams where I meet them and then they tell me they made a mistake. I just… I have to find them." Daisy finally said what had been on her mind. "I need to meet them; I need to know why… It just feels like I can't accept it or move past it until I know. Will you help me?"

Sarah's eyes widened for a moment. "Daisy, understand that sometimes those records are sealed. I can try to help you, but I can't promise anything. Have you spoken to Celia or Lucas about this?"

"Nee." Daisy shook her head. "They won't understand."

Sarah searched her gaze for a long moment before she spoke. "I'll help you as best I can, but you have to promise me two things. First, you're going to talk to Celia and Lucas. They're your familye–your real familye–they deserve to know. And second, you won't get your hopes up for a fairytale reunion. Sometimes it's best not to know, but if you want to know, consider the circumstances around your birth might have been complicated… painful for your birth parents. They might not welcome you with open arms."

Daisy nodded. She had had enough time to consider all the outcomes of her request. "I know, and I promise to do both things, but this is something I have to do."

Their gazes held and a silent agreement came to be. Daisy felt relieved just knowing that she had taken the first step. It will take time for her to learn more, but until then, at least she had hope of finding her birth parents.

Chapter 4
Not the Right Fit

Daisy waited until Sarah went to read to her mother before she asked Celia and Lucas for a moment of their time.

"Is something wrong?" Celia asked, instantly concerned by Daisy's request.

"Nee." Daisy said quickly.

Lucas took a seat at the table and frowned at his youngest sister. "What do you need to talk to us about?"

Daisy had always been the youngest, but in that moment, she felt like a little girl again, over towered by her older brother and big sister.

She let out a quiet sigh before she spoke, her eyes firmly on her hands instead of looking at them. "I've asked Sarah to help me find my birth parents."

"Why would you want to do that?" Celia asked, more confused than angry.

Daisy still didn't look up. She didn't need to see the disappointment in their eyes, she could hear it in their voices. "Because I'm not like you." She got the words out without crying. She looked up and felt a tear slip over her cheek as she met Lucas's gaze. "I can't just pretend it doesn't matter. I can't just go on with my life not knowing where or from whom I came."

"It doesn't matter where or from whom you came, Daisy, it only matters that you're here with us," Celia said calmly, trying to diffuse the situation.

"For you perhaps," Daisy said, shaking her head. "I knew you wouldn't understand. That's why I didn't want to tell you. But I need to know. I need to know why they didn't want me. I need to know why they wanted to give me away instead of keeping me. Didn't I have grandparents that would've taken me in? I need to know who my actual family is."

"We are you actual family. We are your only family," Lucas said through clenched teeth.

Daisy had seen her brother angry before, but she'd never seen him turn that angry gaze on her.

"Are you? Then why don't we look the same? We might be family and we might have been raised as one, but Mamm hardly remembers who we are most days. Maybe I have a real mamm that wants to be part of my life, maybe I want that too," Daisy said, snapping back.

Celia squeezed her hand. "Daisy, what you're saying is hurtful. If Mamm could hear you now. This is your genuine family. She is your real mamm. She wanted you Daisy, she raised you and loved you. If you want to learn about your birth parents, fine. But don't diminish how blessed we were to have Lydia and Noah as our parents." Celia's voice was quiet, but the warning in it was clear.

"Celia's right, Daisy." Sarah's voice spoke behind her. Daisy wasn't sure when Sarah had joined them. It felt wrong for her to step into a family argument, although Daisy knew she was now part of the family.

"Did you encourage her to do this?" Lucas asked with daggers in his eyes.

Sarah shook her head. "Nee, she came to me."

"Well, I don't think any gut can come of this. What if you're hurt by learning the truth? What if they're nothing like you imagined? You have a familye, Daisy, a familye that loves you." Celia insisted.

Daisy had known her brother and sister would guilt her into feeling bad for wanting to find her birth parents. That's why she hadn't told them before now.

But regardless of their warnings and feelings about it, this was something Daisy knew she had to do.

"Don't be angry at Sarah. I only asked if she could help. If she won't help me, then I still intend to find them on my own. I have the copy of the adoption papers you got in Harrisburg and my birth certificate; I'll find a way," Daisy persisted with determination.

She silently prayed that her brother and sister would see that this was something she needed to do, but they looked at her as if she had just grown a second head.

"Why does this matter so much to you?" Celia asked quietly.

Daisy shrugged. "I don't know. I just know that it does."

"Daisy, please…. You've always been a little impulsive. You can't be impulsive with something like this. You'll only get hurt and we'll be left to pick up the pieces."

"And you're too busy with new wife to pick up any pieces of mine." Daisy knew she was being childish, but only because Lucas refused to understand.

"That's not the truth," Lucas's voice filled the kitchen.

"Daisy, you're like a schweschder to me. I didn't marry Lucas to take him away from you," Sarah said in a hurtful tone.

Daisy closed her eyes and took a deep breath. She knew that nothing she could say would make them understand.

Their adoptions and actual parents didn't matter to them, they didn't understand how she felt. Celia was content being a housekeeper and caring for their mother. Lucas had a wife and a farm he wished to build a new life on.

They weren't at odds end with whom they were or what they wanted. How could Daisy ever know what she wanted without knowing why she wasn't wanted in the first place? She summoned a smile and shook her head.

"I'm sorry. It was foolish of me. You're right, it's a ferhoodled thing to do. I'm sorry for upsetting you." The words tasted bitter on her lips. It was the first time in her nineteen years that Daisy had outright lied to her family.

"Gut, you were scaring me." Celia smiled with relief.

"We love you, and that didn't change just because we learned we were adopted. This, here, this is your *real familye*," Lucas offered with a smile that spoke of peace.

Daisy nodded. "Denke. I think I'll turn in."

Daisy rushed to her room and closed the door. For the first time since learning about her adoption, she allowed the tears to come.

She felt lost, lonely, and confused, and the worst part was that she felt as if the people that were her *genuine family* didn't understand her at all.

As if they didn't even want to try.

She knew that her mother would've advised her to pray about her troubles if she had known how upset Daisy was, but Daisy was too upset to even pray.

How could she ask Gott for guidance, when he had guided her actual mother to give her away as if she were a shirt that didn't fit?

Chapter 5
Now We Pray

"Shouldn't Daisy be up already? I know it's a school holiday, but she can't sleep her days away," Lucas commented after his second cup of coffee the following morning.

Celia shrugged. "I thought I'd let her lie in. She's usually up so early and out of the house before the chores even begin. I thought she might deserve a little lie in."

"She was quite upset last night; I don't imagine she slept restfully. Let her sleep in Lucas. It won't do any harm," Sarah agreed.

Celia continued to fry the bacon in one pan whilst frying eggs in the other. Although her brother now had a wife that could cook for him, Celia didn't mind. She enjoyed cooking, especially breakfast. It gave her time to catch up with everyone and to start the day off on a good foot.

She intended to apologize to Daisy this morning for not being more understanding last night. After praying over the matter, she had concluded that although she and Lucas were trying to protect Daisy, it wasn't their place to judge how she should process the news of her adoption.

They could support her if she got hurt, but they couldn't keep her from learning the truth about her birth parents.

"Do you have a lot to do on the farm today?" Sarah asked Lucas as Celia set down a plate in front of each of them.

Celia enjoyed being witness to their new marriage. It was good to see how they talked about their days. Sarah encouraged Lucas with his work on the farm and Lucas supported Sarah's work at social services in town.

One day, Celia hoped to find someone that would be as supportive and encouraging to her as well. But that day was far in the future.

Celia had no intention of searching for love, and while she was taking care of their mother, there wasn't time to find it either.

"I'll be back a little later than usual today. I offered to help with the soup kitchen. It just breaks my heart to see how many people have to come to us for food," Sarah explained, before crunching on a piece of bacon.

Celia nodded as she set down Daisy's plate on the table. "You're an angel for doing what you do. I'd like to offer to cook for the soup kitchen sometime if you'd like?"

"That would be wunderbar," Sarah smiled brightly.

Celia glanced at Lucas's plate, noticing it was nearly empty. She might have allowed Daisy to sleep in, but she wasn't letting anyone out of the house this morning before she was certain there was no residual anger from the night before.

Excusing herself, she made her way to Daisy's room, knocking twice before opening the door. "Daisy, time to turn your face to the sun…" Celia's usual greeting trailed off when she noticed the bed was made, the curtains wide open.

She closed her eyes, trying to remember if Daisy had mentioned going somewhere this morning, but she couldn't remember her having said anything.

Her heart stopped for a moment as she caught sight of the closet and the lack of Daisy's suitcase on top of it. "Nee…."

Celia rushed to the closet and flung open the doors, only to find it empty.

Her breath caught even as she caught sight of the envelope on the bedside table. Her heart sank to the floorboards beneath her feet as she moved to retrieve it.

You are my familye, but I need to find out who I was before I became an Eymann. I promise I'll come home once I have the answers I seek.

Celia, take care of Mamm and don't fret about me too much.

Lucas, don't be angry. Please try to understand.

Sarah, denke for understanding and being willing to help. Tell Mamm I'll be back soon.

Celia wordlessly walked into the kitchen and set the letter down between Lucas and Sarah. Sarah gasped with horror at the words. Lucas let out a frustrated sigh.

"What are we going to do?" Celia asked, concerned for her little sister. Daisy might be a grown woman, but that didn't mean she was ready to face the Englisch world on her own.

"Nothing," Lucas said, shaking his head. "It's too late now. We should've listened last night. Now we pray," Lucas said firmly.

Sarah glanced first at Celia before turning to her husband. "This is why I offered to help her. When she spoke to me, she was so upset… I was afraid she would do something like this…"

"Why didn't you tell me?" Lucas asked.

Sarah shook her head. "She tried to tell you last night."

No one knew better than Celia that it was too late now for regrets. Daisy had left to find her birth parents and even if they went after her now, Celia knew Daisy wouldn't come home before she had the answers she wanted.

Her sister's stubbornness had always infuriated her, but Celia had never for a second imagined that Daisy would simply leave without saying goodbye.

She glanced at Lucas and nodded with a heavy heart. "Now we pray."

Chapter 6
The Most Important Ingredient

Daisy looked back at the town of Mill Creek as the bus pulled away from the curb. Her heart was heavy for not having said goodbye, but she knew she had done the right thing.

Last night she had climbed into bed, but again the nightmares had woken her. This time she had dreamed that her mother was searching for her in the night, calling out her name again and again. But Daisy couldn't find her. When she finally rushed into the cornfields, she came across a woman.

Only it wasn't Lydia Eymann, it was her birthmother.

When she'd woken up in the middle of the night, cold from sweat and quivering from the nightmare, she'd known there was only one thing she could do.

She had to leave without telling her family of her plans. Daisy knew they would try to stop her if she did.

She'd packed her bags and walked all the way to the bus stop. As the sun had made its ascent over the emeralds hills of Lancaster County, Daisy had counted all the money she had saved in her money tin.

She had considered paying for a driver to take her to Harrisburg, but since he didn't know how long or how far her journey would take her, she had waited for the bus instead.

For the last hour, her eyes kept darting back and forth towards the road leading to their community, expecting her brother to come charging into town and demanding her to come home. But luckily, the bus had arrived before Lucas did.

Her only regret was not saying goodbye to her mother.

She turned forward and glanced out the large panorama window of the bus, gazing mindlessly into the distance. She wasn't sure where she was going, but she knew she wouldn't return to Mill Creek until she knew why her birth mother had given her away.

In the time she had spent at the bus stop, another thought had occurred to her. What if her birth mother hadn't given her away? What if she'd been taken away? Was that why she kept dreaming about finding her?

Daisy wasn't sure what she was going to learn about her past, but she knew she had to at least try.

The bus arrived in Harrisburg a little after ten o'clock. Daisy was eager to get started on her journey for the truth. With only enough clothes for a few days, her bible, and her purse, she had little luggage. It was still too much to explore Harrisburg on foot with.

She calculated how much money she had left and decided it would be more than enough for a cab driver in the city. If she was careful, she could pay for a room and feed herself for a week in Harrisburg, before she needed to return home.

Now she just hoped a week was enough to find the answers she wanted.

She watched an Englisch woman flag down a cab driver and did the same. She stepped up to the curb and held her hand in the air. "Taxi!"

Instead of a car pulling over, one pulled up from where it had been parked only a few yards away.

"Need a ride, miss?" The driver leaned over with a friendly smile and a kind expression. He looked to be a year or two older than Daisy.

For a moment she hesitated, having remembered how her family had warned her against strange men when she'd come on Rumspringa a couple of years ago. Fear shot through her like intravenous fluid before she calmed her racing heart.

If she was going to accomplish what she came to the city to do, she had to be brave and pray that Gott would protect her. "Jah, denke," Daisy said, jutting out her chin. "Do you know where social services are?"

The man shrugged before he answered. "Not really, but that's why I have a navigation system. Need help with your bag?"

Daisy shook her head. "Nee, I'll manage. Denke." She climbed into the back seat with her suitcase on the seat beside her. "Is it far?"

She watched as the man punched a few buttons on his phone before he turned to her. "Not at all, about ten minutes away."

Daisy glanced at the rate per mile on the dashboard, pleased that it was less than she would've imagined. "Very well."

The driver pulled into traffic with ease. He navigated through traffic lights, keeping his speed to a minimum the whole time. Daisy was grateful that she didn't feel her life was in danger once during the ride to social services.

"I'm Ryan, by the way," he said over his shoulder a few minutes into the ride. "I've been in that area quite a few times, but I've never noticed the social services building."

"I've never been," Daisy replied without thought. "I'm Daisy. Daisy Eymann."

"Ryan Ascot, it's a pleasure to meet you, Daisy. Are you in town for the day?" Ryan asked, glancing over his shoulder again.

Daisy nodded. She wasn't sure how familiar she should become with her cab driver, but right now he was the only person she knew. "I'm not sure yet."

"Seems like a long way to come, not to be sure how long you'll be coming for," Ryan commented before he turned right onto a side street.

"It depends on what I learn at social services," Daisy explained.

"You see that place over there? Best pizza in the city." Ryan pointed to a restaurant on the side of the road. "Do you eat pizza?"

Daisy couldn't help but laugh. "Jah, of course I eat pizza. We have a nice shop in Mill Creek that sells it. We don't make it at home though..."

"Then you know what the secret ingredient is, right?" Ryan asked over his shoulder.

Daisy was grateful for the small talk. It allowed her to forget about her troubles for a few minutes. "Nee, flour?" she asked, indulging him.

"Flour? Not at all," Ryan chuckled. His laughter made her feel a little more relaxed. "Cheese, it's always cheese!"

Daisy felt a smile curve her mouth. "You're right, the cheese is the most important ingredient."

"Flour too," Ryan conceded.

They shared a smile in the mirror before Ryan turned again. Daisy sat back and watched the large buildings go by, feeling her nerves coil tightly in her belly.

What if she came all this way, and she learned nothing more than she already knew?

Chapter 7
Rock Bottom

Ryan Ascot glanced in the rearview mirror, curious about the Amish girl in the back seat. As a cab driver in Harrisburg, he'd given a few Amish people a ride in the past, but never one that looked as beautiful, determined, or terrified as Daisy Eymann.

He had learned early on that the best cab driver was a quiet one. One who didn't ask questions, who didn't comment on conversations and who turned a blind eye when his back seat was used for a kiss or two. Those were the traits that got him the most tips.

The only reason he had conversed with Daisy was his curiosity. That and the fact that he knew she wouldn't be tipping him.

But now, after having talked to her for a few minutes, his curiosity was even more piqued, and the prospect of not being tipped didn't bother him at all.

Ryan never imagined he would become a cab driver; this wasn't the life he had envisioned for himself when he was younger. But now, he lived through the eyes and experiences of his passengers.

He allowed himself to imagine that he was the weary traveler that had just returned from a trip around the world.

Or the successful businessman rushing from his office to an important meeting at an exclusive restaurant.

He imagined himself to be the father who stopped on his way home to buy his daughter a teddy bear, or the young man that couldn't stop talking about how he had just landed his dream job.

Because the truth of the matter was, Ryan's dreams had been ripped away two years ago.

He could still remember the exact moment he'd learned of his father's suicide. He could remember what he'd worn, where he'd been, and how he had walked out of the admissions office of the college knowing that it had irrevocably changed his life.

Ryan glanced in the rearview mirror at Daisy and saw she was looking out the window. He slowed into traffic and allowed himself to return to the events that had led him to this exact moment.

When his mother had been diagnosed with cancer when Ryan was fourteen, he had believed it would be something she would beat.

She would lose her hair and become very ill before the treatments would work, and then she would be the way she was before the cancer ravaged her body.

That was what his parents had told him.

That was what his mother had promised him.

But things didn't turn out that way at all. Instead, the cancer had ravaged its way through his mother's entire body. Treatment after treatment, she had fought it with everything she had.

If Ryan had seen his father worry about the cost of the treatments a time or two, he hadn't been too concerned.

After all, his father had been a successful investment banker. He earned a pretty penny.

Only, his mother didn't get better and the treatments she had in Switzerland cost more than they could afford. His father had sacrificed his brand-new car and Ryan had sacrificed university to make up the costs.

Neither one of them could've known that his mother wouldn't ever return from Switzerland again. Instead, she had been too weak, the cancer too strong.

When Ryan and his father had returned home alone, it had been the dreariest day in the history of Harrisburg. The sky had been overcast, the weather held a chill, and their home had been empty without his mother there to welcome them.

Still, Ryan thought nothing worse could happen.

Until the sheriff had come. Piece by piece, he had watched them carry all their belongings out of the house. He had turned to his father, confused and afraid, only to learn his father had taken out a second mortgage on the house for his mother's treatments.

When that hadn't been enough, he had taken their entire life savings and put it down on a *sure thing* investment.

The investment had been a dead loss.

They were bankrupt, they couldn't even keep the house, or what little furniture the sheriff didn't take. Ryan had seen his father hit rock-bottom, he had tried to console him, to encourage him they would find a way out of the mountain of debt.

His father found a way.

Suicide.

He'd left nothing more than a note to explain his actions.

Sorry.

A chill ran down Ryan's spine. Even now, two years later, he still couldn't believe his father had chosen the easy way out of an impossible situation. His feelings towards his father see-sawed between anger and disappointment.

It had taken him six months to deal with his father's affairs. He'd walked out broke with nothing but his clothes and his father's second-hand car to remind him of the life he used to have.

The only job he was qualified for immediately: a cab driver.

Ryan had applied the very next day.

He didn't make a great living, but he could afford to pay the rent for his bachelor apartment on the cheaper side of town. He could afford to eat, and he could afford to keep up the maintenance on his car.

The traffic moved slowly as they passed the courthouse. Ryan should've known to take a different route. "Court's just come out probably. That's the only time this road is so busy," he said into the rearview mirror.

Daisy simply nodded.

Ryan realized why he had thought of his father the moment Daisy had climbed into his car. She had that same forlorn, lost look in her eyes as her father had had in the days before he ended his life.

Ryan couldn't have done anything for his father, because he didn't recognize the signs, but he recognized them now.

Ryan wasn't sure why, especially since he didn't know Daisy from a bar of soap, but instinctively he wanted to help her. The traffic eased and a few minutes later, Ryan pulled up in front of the social services building. "Here we are."

Daisy glanced up at the tall building with fear in her eyes. For a brief second, Ryan considered offering to go with her. Knowing that would only frighten her of him, instead he did something else. "Would you like me to wait for you? That way, you don't have to get another ride when you're done?"

Daisy hesitated for a moment. "How much do you charge if you wait?"

Ryan shrugged, recognizing the look. She had little money. "Nothing, it's a quiet day. I don't mind. You can even leave your bag in the back if you want?"

She glanced at her bag before she met Ryan's gaze in the rearview mirror. "Denke. I'm not sure how long I'll be, but I'll try to be quick."

"No problem," Ryan returned with a smile. He watched her head into the building and wondered what could be so important in there for her to have come all the way from Lancaster County.

Chapter 8
Early Bird Gets the Worm

If Daisy had thought that a visit to Harrisburg would solve all her problems, she'd been wrong. Instead, she had run straight into a brick wall by the name of red tape.

After all but begging to see her adoption records, someone had finally shown her to a supervisor who explained it simply wasn't possible.

Not in the state of Pennsylvania.

She walked to the cab, grateful to see that Ryan Ascot hadn't taken off with her suitcase, and climbed in before letting out a quiet sigh.

"Everything all right?" Ryan asked over his shoulder.

Daisy wasn't about to tell a perfect stranger about how she was trying to find her birth parents. Right now, she was confused enough without trying to relay the confusion and red tape to someone else. "Jah... It's fine. Denke for waiting."

Glancing out the window at the tall building, she thought about what she was going to do. She hadn't planned on going further than Harrisburg, but it was clear she would not find the answers she was looking for here.

She thought about how much money she had and debated with herself if it would be enough.

After about five minutes, she realized the car hadn't moved. She looked up, only to see Ryan patiently waiting for her to tell him where to go. "Ach, I'm sorry. I'm distracted. You probably want to get back to work. I can climb out here."

Ryan shook his head. "For what? You don't have any further business here, do you?"

Daisy shook her head, struggling to find a flicker of hope in the darkness. Why had she come on this journey alone? It would've been so much easier with Lucas or Celia telling her what she should do next.

In that moment, Daisy realized that for her entire life until this moment she had looked to her siblings for guidance. She had done this on her own, which meant she had to decide for herself, not for the greater good.

She squared her shoulders and met Ryan's gaze. "Is there a motel nearby? An… affordable one? Preferably one that sells food or has a diner close by?"

Ryan nodded as he switched on the car. "I know just the one. Only a few blocks over and there's a diner right beside it. It's not the Hilton but the sheets are clean, the rate's fair, and the place doesn't smell like stale smoke."

Daisy didn't understand half of what he meant, but she nodded gratefully. "Do you know it?"

Ryan shrugged. "I live there."

Her brow furrowed as fear crept up her spine. Her eyes must've widened with horror because Ryan laughed. "Don't worry, I'm not luring you there with evil intentions. I rent a room by the month. Cheaper than an apartment and since the owner can't drive anymore, he gives me a discount for driving him around."

Relief washed over her. "That's gut to know."

"And if you need a ride in the morning, I'm at your service," Ryan returned with a smile.

Daisy felt the tension ease from her shoulders now that the next twenty hours of her life had at least been planned. She could have something to eat and spend the evening thinking about what she wanted to do next. "How far is it to Millersburg, Ohio?"

Ryan thought for a moment. "About five, six hours' drive. Why?"

"Just wondering if I'm heading there tomorrow. It seems... I need to go there if I want the answers I need. They couldn't help me here," Daisy explained vaguely.

"I can drive you," Ryan said with his eyes on the road. He mentioned a rate and explained that if she covered his meals, he could bring it down a little more.

Daisy thought for a moment and quickly did the math in her head. She could pay Ryan to drive her there and back and still have enough left for a few nights in a motel and her bus fare back to Lancaster County.

But... it was her life's savings.

It was money she had saved over the years from selling her embroidery. She wasn't a master quilter like Celia, but she did a fair job with embroidering names, flowers, or even pretty patterns.

When she helped Celia with embroidering her quilts, Celia always gave her a percentage of the profit as well.

She had saved it to buy her trousseau when she got married one day and now, she was spending it for an entirely different reason completely.

For a moment, she wondered if she wasn't wasting her money on answers she didn't need.

The pounding headache in her skull was a quick reminder of the nightmares that kept robbing her of her sleep. She might not have intended for her savings to be used on a wild goose chase after her birth parents, but if it meant she could move on with her life without wondering about the past, then it would be worth every single penny.

"Are you free to go to Millersburg tomorrow? We might be there for a day or two," Daisy asked, satisfied with her decision.

Ryan's mouth curved into a smile. "I've been itching to drive long distance for a while. It'll be fun."

Daisy wasn't sure about the fun part, but Ryan's excitement at least made her laugh. "Gut, we can leave at seven o'clock if that suits you?"

Ryan's eyes widened. "Early bird gets the worm?"

Daisy shook her head. "I'm a teacher's assistant. Classes start at seven. I'm an early riser."

"Then tomorrow, I'll be an early riser too," Ryan promised as he turned into the parking of lot of a motel. Just like he promised, it looked neat, affordable, and welcoming. "Let's get you checked in."

Chapter 9
You Won't Score
Unless You Shoot

The following morning Ryan grabbed his coffee to-go from the diner, before he went to wait for Daisy by the car. He wasn't sure how she took her coffee, so he asked for cream and sugar, hoping she wouldn't mind.

After getting her checked in last night, he had spent the rest of the evening wondering why an Amish girl would visit social services only to go to Millersburg the next day. Ryan wasn't curious by nature about his passengers, but something about Daisy intrigued him.

He had a strong need to help her, although he wasn't sure what he was helping her with. Instead of watching television like he did most nights, he'd spent his evening researching the Amish on the internet.

 Nothing he had learned about them explained Daisy's visit to Harrisburg or her intentions to go to Millersburg.

Ryan had considered that she might be visiting family, but if she was visiting family, why would she ask him if he minded staying a day or two? Did she want a getaway car if she didn't like them, or didn't she plan on seeing family at all?

The questions keep mounting in his mind and they had a long road ahead of them today. Just perhaps, he could try to find some answers on the way.

Daisy locked her room at exactly ten minutes to seven. Ryan watched as she walked to the office to return the key, before she approached him with her suitcase in hand. Her face looked fresh, her hair neatly tied back beneath her bonnet. For a moment, Ryan could imagine himself to be in a different century as he watched her stop beside him.

"Guten Mayrie, Ryan. Denke for being on time," Daisy greeted him with a smile.

Yesterday her smile had been pretty, but something about it this morning made his heart skip a beat. Her eyes seemed bluer than the day before, her features more alluring. Ryan cleared his throat and held out a take-out cup. "Morning, I got you coffee. It's got cream and sugar; I hope you don't mind." Ryan frowned when her eyes widened with surprise. "Wait, don't you drink coffee?"

Daisy's laughter was light. "Of course I drink coffee. How else do you think I spend all day running after kinner? Denke, the sugar and cream are both welcome."

Ryan flashed her a grin of relief. "Great, ready to get on the road?"

Daisy nodded.

Ryan put her suitcase in the trunk this time. When she opened the back door, he stopped it with his hand. "Since we're going to be on the road for a good five or six hours, wouldn't you rather ride up front?"

Daisy nodded in agreement. Ryan couldn't be more grateful that he'd taken the time to clean out the front seat before she arrived.

Soon they were driving through morning traffic towards the highway that would take them to Ohio. Daisy was quiet beside him, sipping on her coffee while she watched the buildings pass her by through the window.

Ryan waited until they were clear of the city before he turned to her with a curious look. "What's in Millersburg?"

Daisy looked at him with a look of hesitation.

"Don't worry, if you don't want to tell me, you don't have to. I know it's rude to pry. I'm just curious by nature," Ryan quickly offered.

Daisy was quiet for a few moments before she let out a quiet sigh. "It's not a big secret, it's just that I don't even know if I'm going to find what I'm looking for."

"What are you looking for?" Ryan flinched. "Scratch that, sorry."

Daisy's laughter was sweet, filling the inside of his car with happy vibes. Ryan glanced at her from the corner of his eye and felt his heart skip a beat. She was really pretty, much prettier than he'd realized.

"It's all right, I'll tell you. I guess it's only right, since you're the one driving me," Daisy said when her laughter subsided. "I found out six months ago that I was adopted."

"That's... I'm not sure if I should say I'm happy for you or if I'm sorry to hear that..." Ryan said awkwardly. There wasn't really social protocol for someone making a statement like that.

"I'm not sure which it is either. Until six months ago, I was happy and content with my life and now… I'm not even sure who I really am," Daisy admitted. He could hear the doubt in her voice, just as he could hear the uncertainty.

"Did your adopted parents treat you well?" Ryan could kick himself. He really needed to stop asking stupid questions.

"They treated me wonderfully. I was raised in a loving home, filled with laughter, acceptance, and love. I never once suspected that I didn't belong, not even because my hair is red and theirs isn't. It just didn't occur to me. Until my mamm said something she shouldn't have…" Daisy turned and glanced out the window as she continued to talk. "You see, she has Alzheimer's. She gets confused sometimes. Other times she's as clear as a whistle. But one day… she told my bruder that she couldn't have kinner. My bruder said there was something about her voice that made him realize she wasn't just confused…"

With his eyes on the road, Ryan listened. Here and there he struggled to understand the Pennsylvania Dutch that mingled with her Englisch, but he understood well enough to get the gist of it.

"Lucas, my bruder, finally found out that we were all adopted. All three of us. He insisted it didn't matter, that Lydia and Noah were the only parents that mattered. Because they wanted us… But… I don't know… I just feel as if I need to know more. Celia, my older schweschder, she says the only family that matters is the one she had now, but I can't just forget about being adopted…" Daisy sighed heavily. "They're angry at me for wanting to know."

"Maybe they just don't understand?" Ryan offered hopefully. It was clear from the way she spoke of her family that they were very close. Ryan could understand how her family, especially her parents, could feel offended by her wanting to find her birth parents. "What does your father say?"

"My daed died ten years ago. And with mamm…. She can't really answer the questions I have. Besides, the last thing I want to do is to upset her when she has a clear moment. They're become fewer and fewer these days."

"I'm sorry to hear that." Ryan could imagine how lost and confused she must feel. Without her parents explaining to her, she had been left to come to her own conclusions. "And Celia and Lucas don't want to know about their birth parents?"

"Nee. Lucas just got married and Celia says learning about the past might just be more painful that it is reassuring." Daisy shook her head and turned to him. "Do you think so?"

"That the past might be more painful that reassuring? Yeah, I do." Ryan nodded soberly, thinking about his own past. There was nothing reassuring left in his past. The memories had of his parents before the cancer came and ruined it all were fading a little more with time. He could only hope that they didn't fade away completely. "So are your birth parents in Millersburg?"

"I don't know," Daisy admitted. "The lady in Harrisburg said she couldn't help me. They seal all the adoption records between states. If I want to find out who they are, I need to go to Millersburg, where the adoption was filed. Apparently, Ohio unsealed their records as of 1996."

"And if you can find your unsealed adoption records, then you'll know who your birth parents are." Ryan finished, understanding why they were going to Millersburg.

"Jah. But only if my birth parents gave permission for me to contact them one day. If they didn't... then we would've driven all this way for nothing," Daisy shrugged with defeat.

Ryan knew that the chances of her finding their names were a long shot in the dark, but he had to admire her for trying. "You won't score a basket unless you shoot."

"What?" Daisy turned to him, confused.

Ryan chuckled, realizing she wouldn't understand the nod to basketball. "It means that if you don't try, you won't know. At least you're trying."

Daisy smiled. "Jah, at least I'm trying."

"Do you get along with your brother and sister?" Ryan asked, eager to learn more about her family. He wanted to know everything he could about her. Perhaps then he'd understand the need to want to help her.

Or why he his heart skipped a beat whenever she smiled at him.

"It's a gut thing we've got a long road ahead, because that's going to take a while to explain." Daisy smiled lightheartedly as she talked about her siblings.

As he listened about her brother teasing her and how her brother and sister ganged up on her when they were younger, Ryan realized that there wasn't once regret or sadness in her voice. She spoke of her childhood with dearness and affection, humor and sibling rivalry.

Ryan couldn't help but realize that although she hadn't been born into the Eymann family, Daisy had struck gold to have Celia and Lucas as her siblings and her adopted parents as a mother and a father.

Her childhood sounded pretty perfect to a person standing on the outside looking in.

Especially for a person who had no family at all.

Chapter 10
Bobblehead Bamboozle

Daisy felt a little apprehensive as Ryan stopped in front of another tall building. Only this time, they were in Millersburg.

The road had been long, but to her curious mind, it had been quite the adventure. She'd seen small towns, farmlands, mountains, and then watched as the landscape changed once again before they arrived in the city of Millersburg.

To Daisy, all cities looked the same. There were no trees, no fields, and no fresh air. They consisted of concrete and tall buildings that blocked out the sun.

Sidewalks littered with papers snaked along the sides of the road. The air smelled like burnt coal or fuel; it was nothing like the fresh air she was used to in Mill Creek.

"Would you like me to come with you this time?" Ryan offered as he switched off the car.

Daisy turned to him with a moment's hesitation. Ryan was no longer a stranger to her, instead he'd become almost a friend over the last two days. He was the only person she had confessed to about her true feelings about her adoption.

Right now, he was the only person there to support her.

"Jah, if you don't mind, I'd like that very much." Daisy finally answered. She wasn't sure what she was going to find when she found someone willing to help her. Perhaps it might be good to have an Englischer there if the person was biased because of her religion.

"Sure," Ryan smiled before he climbed out of the car.

Together they headed inside, where Daisy explained her problem to a woman that approached them. They were told to be seated until someone was free to help them.

While they waited, Daisy watched people come and go. This was a place where help could be found or offered. Some came to beg for more visitation rights, others came to plead to get their children back after the state had taken them away.

After two hours, Daisy wasn't only hungry, but she was losing hope that anyone was ever going to help her. She quietly prayed that Gott would guide her journey and would send someone kind and willing to help her when someone called her name.

"Miss Eymann?" a woman called out from an office a few yards away.

"That's us," Daisy said, standing up.

Ryan followed her to the woman's office, where they were welcomed inside.

"I see you'd like to find your adoption records?" the woman asked, not bothering to introduce herself.

"Jah," Daisy nodded. "All I have are the official documents that confirm my parents adopted me and my original birth certificate. I'm hoping to locate my birth parents. I was told in Harrisburg that Ohio's records have been unsealed, that you can help me?" Daisy asked hopefully.

The woman didn't answer, instead she rudely tapped on a keyboard, keeping her eyes on her screen.

Daisy glanced at Ryan. He shrugged showing he didn't know why she was being so rude.

Finally, she turned to them again with a cocked brow. "Just because Ohio unsealed adoption records after 1994, doesn't mean that everyone has access to them. For me to give you the names of your birth parents, they would've needed to consent to revealing it to you when the time came."

Ryan sat forward in his seat, leaning with his elbow on the table as he listened closely.

"What does that mean?" Daisy asked, confused. "I was told you could help me."

"Yes, and if your birth parents consented to me revealing their names, I could've. But they didn't, so I can't." She shrugged, making it clear she had nothing else to say.

Ryan stood up and moved around the woman's desk. "Is this a Darius Miles Bobblehead?"

Daisy frowned, slightly irritated that Ryan was more concerned with the ornaments in the woman's office than he was with her problem.

The woman smiled for the first time since they had entered her office. "Yes, it is. I'm a big Clippers fan, you?"

"Huge!" Ryan said, holding his hands apart to indicate size. "Do you go see them often?"

Ryan leaned against the chest of drawers behind her, talking to her as if she was his new best friend.

Daisy wasn't sure if it was jealousy or anger, but she didn't like the way Ryan smiled at the woman.

The woman laughed. "Often, every single game. My husband buys season tickets."

"That's sounds awesome," Ryan agreed enthusiastically. He shook the doll so that the head bobbed up and down.

Daisy could strangle him for drawing her attention away from her dilemma with questions about dolls. "As I was saying, isn't there…"

Ryan cut her off. "Well, it was really nice of you to look and we understand your hands are tied. Say, do you know any nice motels in the area? Affordable but clean?"

"I do, the Bell Hop Inn. It's not too far and in a quiet area. Did you come from far?" the woman asked Ryan, much friendlier than she had been with Daisy.

"Harrisburg. Anyway, thanks for your time. And enjoy your next game." Ryan returned the bobblehead to its place before he moved around the desk and smiled at Daisy. "You coming?"

Daisy was all but fuming by the time they reached the car. She climbed in and slammed the door so hard that if Ryan had any doubt about her opinion of his actions, he didn't anymore.

As soon as he was in the car, she turned to him with anger blazing in her eyes. "You realize we came all this way and instead of helping me to get the names of my birth parents, you stood there talking about football."

"Basketball," Ryan shrugged, reaching for a piece of paper on the dashboard. "Do you have a pen?"

Daisy reached into her purse and handed him one. "We came all this way for nothing. How am I ever going to find out who my birth parents were now? She said they didn't consent to me ever learning their names... what kind of parents do that?"

"The... Rowena Bartley type," Ryan said, handing her the piece of paper. "That's the name of the woman listed as your natural mother."

"What?" Daisy asked, confused.

Ryan chuckled. "Daisy, I wasn't talking to her about basketball because I was interested. I needed to find a way behind the desk to see what was on her computer. She had your records open on the screen. There wasn't a name listed as natural father, but that name," Ryan tapped the name on the piece of paper in Daisy's hand, "that's your mother."

Daisy's eyes widened as she realized what Ryan had done. "You did that for me?"

"It was clear she didn't want to help you. You could've begged and she still would've thrown the book at you."

"Why would she have thrown a book at me?" Daisy asked, perplexed.

Ryan smiled at her with indulgence. "It's a figure of speech, meaning she wasn't willing to help you, regardless of how important it was. So I got you what you need."

"Rowena Bartley...." Daisy said the name slowly. It sounded foreign, not like family at all. "How do we find her?"

Ryan started the car and pulled into traffic. "We find the Bell Hop Inn, check in for the evening and then we find somewhere quiet to eat—I'm starving. Then, after I'm fed, we'll do some research on the internet and see how many Rowena Bartleys live in the area."

"You can do that?" Daisy asked, surprised. She knew technology was powerful and informative. She didn't imagine it could track down someone you were looking for.

"Sure, but first food." Ryan smiled.

Daisy nodded with a grateful smile. "Denke Ryan. Gott truly blessed me when he sent you to pick me up."

"We haven't found her yet; you can thank me then." Ryan winked at her before turning back to the road.

Chapter 11
Chicken Fried Steak

The Bell Hop Inn was just like the lady at social services had described. It was clean, affordable, and luckily, had rooms available for the night. Ryan insisted he would pay for his own room, but Daisy refused.

After his stunt at social services, she seemed even more hopeful than before about finding her birth parents. They walked about a mile before they found a restaurant that wasn't too commercial, and that offered free Wi-Fi.

They each ordered a chicken fried steak with a side order of vegetables and a milkshake. Ryan could feel the other restaurant guests curiously looking over at their table time and time again, but they didn't bother him.

He understood their curiosity about a normal guy sitting with an Amish girl. He would've been curious as well.

Instead, between bites, he focused on tracking down Rowena Bartley.

"Celia's is better," Daisy muttered as she set down her fork. "I'm sorry, I shouldn't have said that. There are people suffering from hunger and here I am ungrateful for the chicken fried steak."

Ryan frowned. "This chicken fried steak is pretty much the best I've ever had?"

Daisy shook her head and leaned forward. "Celia makes her batter different. It's crunchy and salty while the steak is still tender. This one is a little tough." Daisy finished in barely more than a whisper.

Ryan chuckled. "Sounds amazing. Aaah, I found her," Ryan frowned, "or should I say them?"

"Them?" Daisy asked, confused.

"Four, to be exact. Within the town of Millersburg and area there are four Rowena Bartleys. Two of them are married and now go by different surnames," Ryan explained.

"You can find all that on your phone?" Daisy asked, flabbergasted.

Ryan nodded. "Yeah, on the internet. It's like a library, but it's free and anyone can access it. People share their photos, their telephone numbers, and, in this case, the town registry, and then you can find it online if you know how to look."

"And you know how to look," Daisy nodded. "Would you mind staying another day? I know you're probably in a hurry to get back to Harrisburg and your life there, but I wouldn't feel comfortable with another driver..." Daisy trailed off with hope in her eyes.

Ryan nodded with a smile curling the corners of his mouth. How could he deny her when she asked so sweetly?

Besides, he felt invested in this expedition. He was just as curious as Daisy to see if she would find her birth mother.

And if she didn't, Ryan hoped he could be a friend for her to lean on.

"Sure, it's not like I have anyone or anything waiting for me in Harrisburg." He tucked another fry into his mouth and savored the salty taste.

"You don't have familye?" Daisy asked, concerned.

Ryan sighed; his appetite suddenly gone. "Nope. Lost my mom to cancer and my dad… let's just say he wasn't willing stick around after she passed. He…" Ryan swallowed past the lump in his throat. Even two years later, it was still hard for him to talk about. "He took his own life after my mom died. The debt of her treatments… it was a little too much for him to handle."

Daisy's eyes softened with empathy. "Ach, Ryan. I'm so sorry. I can't imagine how hard it must have been for you. To lose first your mamm and then your daed."

"Hard," Ryan smiled sadly. "But hey, at least I'm here and still kicking."

"And helping me," Daisy added with a kind smile.

Ryan nodded. "And helping you."

Daisy held his gaze and for a moment Ryan felt as if he was privileged simply to be in her company. Although she was troubled, she had a way of exuding calm. "Ryan," Daisy said, searching his gaze. "You know that Gott has plans for you? Plans to help you, not to harm you. Regardless of what you've lost, always remember that."

Ryan nodded, feeling a little overwhelmed. He was supposed to be helping her, although he couldn't help but feel as if spending time with Daisy was helping him as well.

He'd never met anyone like her before. She carried her faith like a shining beacon, instead of hiding it beneath modern clothes and political beliefs.

She spoke of God as if he was her friend, instead of the way the priest at Ryan's childhood church used him to threaten his congregation. Daisy might not realize it, but right now she was helping Ryan more than he was helping her.

She was reminding him that there was more to life than just getting by.

There was hope.

Chapter 12
Pauline the Prankster

When Daisy had left her home in the early hours of dawn two days ago, she hadn't even considered what she would feel like when she stood in front of the house of her birth mother.

Possible birth mother, she quickly reminded herself.

Ryan had plotted out a route for them to visit all four addresses he found on the internet today. The first address wasn't too far from the Bell Hop Inn. It had only taken them fifteen minutes to arrive.

Now Daisy was suddenly overwrought with random thoughts racing through her mind. What if Rowena wasn't home? What if her children were home? What if her husband opened the door?

What if she was about to bother a complete stranger who had no relation to the Rowena Bartley they were looking for at all?

"The door will not come any closer," Ryan said quietly by her side.

Last night at dinner, she had thoroughly enjoyed his company. After he told her about his family, Daisy had felt as if she understood him a little better. She sympathized with him losing his parents, and with having no other family in his life.

She couldn't help but feel guilty for leaving her family to find a birth mother that didn't want her in the first place. Like most nights, it had interrupted her sleep with another nightmare.

Only this time Daisy had found her birth mother, only to return home to learn that her adopted mother had passed away when she hadn't been there.

Daisy had woken up overwhelmed with guilt. She wanted nothing more than to call the phone shanty at their neighbor's house to enquire about her mother's well-being, but she wasn't ready to reveal her whereabouts to her siblings just yet.

She knew that if Lucas knew where she was, he would come and get her. Right now, she had to admit that sounded like a wonderful thing. But she couldn't, not until she knew.

Besides, Lucas had a farm to care for and a new wife that needed his attention. This was something she had vowed to do on her own, and now she had to go through with it.

"You don't have to do this if you don't want to. We can get in the car and go back to Harrisburg right now if you'd rather put this all behind you?" Ryan asked, reaching for her hand.

His hand was reassuring and warm. Daisy turned to him, grateful once again that Gott had sent him to join her on this journey. "I need to do this."

Daisy put one foot in front of the other until she stood on the doorstep. She glanced over her shoulder at Ryan before she lifted her hand and knocked.

Her heart was racing a mile a minute, fear gushing through her veins at what might happen next.

When the door opened, a woman was behind it, wearing exercise clothes and holding a purple towel in her hand. "Oh no, don't tell me. You're here to tell me I worship the devil and it's time to see the error of my ways?"

Daisy frowned, confused for a moment before she realized the woman had mistaken her for a door-to-door missionary. "Nee, not at all. I'm looking for a Rowena Bartley?"

The woman's laughter was spontaneous. "Bartley, I haven't owned that name since four last names ago. What do you want with me?"

Daisy's eyes widened, realizing the woman had been married many times. She quickly reminded herself not to judge. Drawing in a steadying breath, she met the woman's gaze. "I know this might sound strange to you, and I'm not trying to offend you, but did you perhaps give up a baby girl for adoption nineteen years ago?"

This time, her laughter was almost hysterical. "Wait, did Pauline put you up to this? I've got to call her. This is the best prank yet."

Daisy shook her head. "I don't know Pauline. Did you?"

As if realizing for the first time Daisy was serious, the woman shook her head. "No, no I'm sorry. I've had no children. You must be looking for someone else."

Daisy nodded, almost relieved that this serial bride in her shocking pink skin tight clothes wasn't her birth mother. "Denke, and sorry for wasting your time."

Daisy walked back to the car and shook her head. Ryan nodded and moved around to climb into the driver's seat. She expected him to sympathize or to tell her it was for the best, but as if he sensed she wasn't sure of her feelings either, he simply turned to her and said; "Onto Rowena Bartley number two."

Chapter 13
A Barn Raising Cult

After driving for about ten minutes, Ryan turned to Daisy, glad to see that her face wasn't drawn with disappointment anymore. It was as if she could process any hardship in a matter of minutes. It was admirable.

"I have to say, I thought you'd be more upset," Ryan commented.

Daisy shrugged. "How can I be upset when it wasn't Gott's will?"

Ryan glanced at her, once again surprised by how easily she spoke of God. "How do you know what his will is?"

Daisy turned to him with an indulgent smile. "I don't, no one does. We only accept it when he reveals it to us."

Ryan thought for a moment before he finally let out a sigh. "How do you know so much about God? Did your parents teach you or is just because you're Amish?"

Daisy laughed softly. "You make it sound like I belong to a cult."

"No, I'm sorry, that's now how I meant it to sound. It's just… I've met no one who refers to their faith as if it were a living part of their lives," Ryan explained.

"That's sad. Because that's exactly what faith is. It guides us, it consoles us, it gives us hope. It should be part of our lives. Isn't it part of yours?" Daisy asked curiously.

Ryan shrugged. "Not like that. Sure, I go to church now and then and when I do, they usually make me feel guilty for not going more often. Then I tend to not go for a while again." Ryan glanced at her before he asked the next question. "Are all Amish like you?"

Daisy thought for a moment before she sighed. "If you mean like me with my clothes and my faith, then jah. But in what I like and what I'm gut at, nee. We're all different people. We just share the same faith, the same congregation, the same ordnung."

"Ordnung?" Ryan cocked a brow.

"The ordnung is how we live… almost like a set of rules, if you want to call it that. Nee, not rules, restrictions," Daisy explained.

"Tell me more about the Amish? All I know is what I've seen on television," Ryan explained.

Daisy spoke with ease as she told him about how faith was the biggest part of their lives. How every decision, every hardship, and every concern was turned over to God for guidance. He learned how community, family, and faith was prioritized before anything else.

"Like if you think of our farms, we don't farm to become wealthy. We farm what we need to farm to make enough profit to last us until the next harvest," Daisy explained.

"And if you make more than you need?" Ryan asked curiously. "Do you buy a new buggy or something?"

Daisy laughed and shook her head. "We don't purchase what we do not need and we purchase nothing that feeds into Hochmuth. *Pride,*" Daisy continued to explain. "For example, we don't have ornaments or wear Englisch clothes, because that would differentiate us from others in our community. Once we differentiate from each other, it won't be long before Hochmuth becomes a part of our lives.

One person will think themselves better for having a nicer piece on their mantel, whereas another might feel more important because his clothes are more expensive.

If we all live by the same means, the same rules, we don't judge and we don't differentiate."

Ryan nodded. It seemed like the perfect way to stop discrimination. No one could be jealous of anyone because of their belongings. "And except for working and praying, what other things do you do... like for fun?"

"A lot of things. We swim in the creek in summer, we have a harvest picnic after the harvest. We have barn raisings—ach you should see how wunderbaar that is. The entire community comes together when we have a barn raising. The planning is done weeks ahead of time by carpenters and men willing to help. Then, on the very day of the barn raising, the whole community comes out. All capable men help with carrying lumber, hammering nails, or any other task that needs to be done, while the women and kinner make sure there's plenty to eat and drink for everyone the entire day. It's a feast," Daisy said, clearly a big supporter of barn raisings.

"Then the person whose barn it is pays everyone for the day's work?" Ryan asked as he turned onto the road where the next Rowena Bartley lived.

"Nee, of course not. No money exchanges hands. We do it as a community, because one day if we're in need, we know the community will do it for us," Daisy explained.

Ryan shook his head. "It sounds almost too good to be true. Do people ever leave?"

"Sometimes, but mostly nee. Usually after Rumspringa, most Amish youngsters return home to be baptized."

"So they have a choice?" Ryan asked, surprised.

"Of course, we have a choice. It's not a cult," Daisy laughed.

Ryan nodded, finally understanding. He'd always thought that the Amish were bound to their communities from birth. He hadn't realized it was an adult decision to stay in the community or leave. He glanced at the numbers of the houses and pulled up beside number 2107.

"Here you are, Rowena Bartley, number two."

Daisy nodded. "Hopefully, this one doesn't laugh at me."

Chapter 14
Rowena Number Two

"I hope she doesn't laugh at me." Daisy said again, feeling the fear return.

"I'm sure she won't," Ryan promised with a smile.

Daisy climbed out and walked up to the gate. She pressed the button for the bell and waited a few moments before the gate slowly opened automatically.

"Go on," Ryan encouraged her.

Daisy drew in a deep breath and approached the front door. Before she could knock, an elderly man opened the door with a curious look. "Did you remember my Lipitor? Last month you forgot it?"

Daisy shook her head. "I'm sorry, I don't understand."

"Cholesterol! Last month you forgot my cholesterol medication," the man said irritably.

Daisy sighed, realizing she was once again being mistaken for someone else. "I'm not here about your medication, sir. I'm looking for Rowena Bartley."

"Rowena? Did you know her?" the man asked with a curious look.

Daisy shook her head, not sure how to answer. "I'm afraid not. Is she home?"

The elderly man's eyes softened as he shook his head. "Rowena passed on, my dear, fifteen years ago. I still miss her every single day."

Daisy felt her hope crashing to the floor. "I see. You wouldn't know if she… if she ever had a child?"

"Yes, of course. We had the twins. Andrew is in banking and Michael is a doctor. I'm sorry, who are you again?" he asked, narrowing his eyes.

Daisy gathered her courage and squared her shoulders. "A Rowena Bartley gave me up for adoption a little over nineteen years ago. I'm trying to find my birth mother."

The man laid a gentle hand on Daisy's shoulder as he searched her eyes. "I'm afraid the Rowena you're looking for wasn't mine. Nineteen years ago Rowena and I were raising six-year-old twins and trying to juggle our careers whilst getting them settled into private school. There is no way Rowena could've been pregnant without me knowing. Besides, Bartley was her married name…"

Daisy nodded, feeling tears burn her eyes. Once again, she had just wasted someone's time with her own wild goose chase.

Instead of chasing after a mother that didn't want her, she should go home and spend time with the mother that raised her.

She swallowed past the lump in her throat and smiled gratefully at the man. "Denke, I'm sorry for bothering you."

"No problem at all. I hope you find what you're looking for," he called after Daisy as she walked out the gate and back to the car.

She couldn't help but wonder at his word choice. Why did he say he hoped she found what she was looking for instead of whom she was looking for?

"Onto Rowena number three?" Ryan asked patiently beside her.

Daisy turned to him, tears burning her eyes as she shook her head. "What am I doing? I'm chasing after a mother who didn't want me. A mother that gave me away like I was a bag of trash she needed to take out. My own familye doesn't even know where I am. They must be worried sick over me and here I am knocking on doors trying to find a woman that didn't want me in the first place?"

Tears streamed over her cheeks as her shoulders shook with emotion.

Ryan wrapped an arm around her shoulder and held her while she cried. "You're doing what you feel is right. This was something you needed to do. You've come this far already. Are you sure you want to stop now? She might be Rowena number three, or Rowena number four… But if you stop now, you'll never know."

Daisy nodded and sniffed back the tears. When she turned and met Ryan's gaze, she realized that with him by her side, she didn't feel alone or afraid.

He had been nothing but kind and patient since he picked her up at the bus stop. What other man would've done the same for her?

She might pay him, but Daisy knew he would make much more driving around in Harrisburg than helping her search for her mother. "Why are you doing this? Why are you so nice to me?"

Ryan used his thumb to brush away a tear before he smiled at her. "Because... because I want to. Spending time with you is the best thing I have done in a while. Because... you opened my eyes after I've been lost in the dark. You just have to keep faith that you'll find her. Like you said, if it isn't God's will, we'll know when we reach number four."

Daisy thought for a moment. She considered going back to Lancaster County and putting all of this behind her, but she only had to remember the nightmares and the feelings of uncertainty to know she couldn't.

She had to finish what she had started.

"Then onto Rowena number three." She offered Ryan a small smile, wondering why the first time she felt attraction towards a man, it was a man she could never fall in love with?

"Onwards we go," Ryan said as he started the engine.

Daisy glanced at him and smiled secretly as she turned to glance out the window. If it wasn't for him, she would've been lost and an emotional wreck.

He might not have faith the same way she did, but he was certainly being guided by Gott.

As she watched the houses go by, Daisy wondered if there were men like Ryan in her community back home. Someone who made her feel at ease, someone who understood her.

A man that made her heart skip a beat, one that could make her smile when she felt sad.

If there was, she hadn't met him yet.

She sneaked a peek at Ryan and wished he had been Amish.

Chapter 15
Faced with Your Past

Ryan stopped in front of the house where Rowena number three presumably lived. He glanced at Daisy and noticed the trepidation in her eyes.

He couldn't be sure if she wanted this to be the house where her birth mother lived or if she just wanted all of this to be over with.

Although he'd only known her a couple of days, he cared for her. At first, he'd thought it was his protective instincts encouraging him to help her.

But after spending the last two days with her, Ryan knew it wasn't just that. Something else about Daisy made him want to spend more time with her.

More time than just the time they would have searching for her birth mother.

Was it wrong if him to hope that this wasn't the house? The right Rowena? Because that would mean they would have a little more time together.

"I guess I should go knock," Daisy said, glancing at the house.

It was a two-story house with blue shutters and a blue front door. To Ryan, it looked like the perfect storybook family home in suburbia. "Would you like me to come with this time?"

Daisy turned to him with a grateful look. "Please, I'm not sure I can face being turned away a third time on my own."

"Sure," Ryan offered her a smile. "Besides, if this is it, I'd like to meet her."

Together, they crossed the perfectly manicured lawn. Like the rest of the yard, they carefully tended the flower beds. Not a single weed in sight. Even the roses seemed controlled, not a single leaf or bloom out of place.

Daisy glanced at him as they reached the front door. "Here I go again."

Ryan knocked twice. "This time, you've got me for backup."

Daisy chuckled. "Denke."

While they waited, Ryan turned to her with a questioning look. "Does your family really not know where you are?"

Guilt flashed in her eyes. "Nee…."

Before she could explain, the door opened. The woman gasped even as her hands flew to her face in surprise when she caught sight of Daisy.

For a moment Ryan was confused before he noticed the woman's strawberry colored hair and striking blue eyes.

Daisy turned to Ryan with a wide-eyed expression, uncertain how to react.

"I'm sorry, forgive me my manners. You just… you reminded of someone… How can I help you?" The woman offered with an apologetic smile, trying to pretend she hadn't just acted as if she'd seen a ghost.

Ryan realized Daisy was as silent as a mouse beside him. He turned to the woman with a hopeful smile. "Hi, I'm Ryan and this is Daisy. We're looking for Rowena Bartley?"

The woman looked at Daisy again and her eyes welled up with tears. "You found me…"

She stepped forward and framed Daisy's face. There was so much emotion in her eyes, Ryan knew he didn't have to say anything else.

"You're the splitting image of me at your age…" Rowena trailed off.

Ryan took a step back, realizing how important this moment was for both women.

"I wasn't sure I was going to find you…" Daisy trailed off, her voice cracking with emotion.

"I wasn't sure I'd ever get to see you again," Rowena sniffed before she pulled Daisy close for a hug.

Ryan felt his own heart swell at the sight. The last time Rowena had seen Daisy, she had been a baby. He could only imagine how wonderful it was for her to see her daughter again.

This was what Daisy had been looking for, to meet the mother that gave her life.

The mother she never had a privilege of knowing.

Rowena stepped back and quickly brushed the tears from her face. Her eyes darted up and down the road before she turned to Ryan and Daisy. "Come inside, please?"

Ryan waited for Daisy's cue.

"I'd like that very much," Daisy said in a small voice.

Ryan followed the ladies inside, hoping that Daisy was going to get the answers she had been looking for.

Chapter 16
Here's Your Hat, What's The Hurry

Daisy looked around the living room, nervously waiting for Rowena to return.

For *her mother* to return.

She couldn't call it a connection, but she felt a type of recognition when she looked at Rowena for the very first time. Perhaps it because they were so alike, Daisy wouldn't know for sure.

Rowena had invited them inside and asked them to wait for her in the living room while she fetched them something to drink.

Daisy wasn't thirsty by any means, but she understood that Rowena perhaps needed a moment to steady her emotions before she talked about her past.

That was why Daisy had come after all. To learn about Rowena's past and the decisions that had led her to giving away her daughter.

"Here we go, I brought us some orange juice. I hope that's all right?" Rowena returned with a tray that held three glasses.

"That's perfect, thanks," Ryan said, accepting a glass.

Daisy accepted hers and couldn't help but be grateful that Ryan was there by her side. She wasn't sure she would've had the courage to come in had it not been for Ryan.

"I still can't get over how much you look like me," Rowena said, shaking her head.

Daisy smiled, noticing the photos on a side table. They were of Rowena, a man Daisy presumed to be her husband, and three children. Two sons and a daughter. The daughter took after Rowena, but not as much as Daisy did.

"Can you tell me anything about my father?" Daisy asked, turning to Rowena.

Rowena let out a heavy sigh. "I should've known you were going to want to know what happened back then. I guess it's only right to tell you."

"If you don't mind?" Daisy asked hopefully.

Ryan nodded. "She's come a long way to find you. It's been quite a journey. Did you know there are four Rowena Bartley's that live in and around Millersburg?"

Rowena shook her head. "No, no I didn't." A frown creased her brow. "I never thought I'd get to meet you. I agreed for the adoption records to be sealed."

Daisy wasn't about to argue, instead she shrugged. "Neither did I."

Rowena held her glass with both her hands, staring into the yellow juice for a few moments before she spoke. "I know nothing about your father, really. It shames me to admit it, but I only met him once. It was spring break and a few of my friends and I were at a party one evening… He was charming. Delightfully so. In fact, he charmed me into sleeping with him." Rowena shook her head. "If only I knew then what I know now. I didn't even know his last name, never saw him again. His name was Timothy."

"Timothy," Daisy muttered the name. She wouldn't judge Rowena for what happened, it wouldn't be right. But she'd hoped to at least know a little more about her father.

"You only found out you were pregnant a few months later?" Ryan prodded her to continue telling her story.

"Yes. At first, I wasn't sure. One of my friends finally convinced me to do a home test… It was positive. I can still remember feeling as if my whole world had just tumbled down around me." Rowena looked at Daisy with a pleading look.

"You have to understand. I was only sixteen years old—barely. I still had my whole life ahead of me."

"Is that when you decided not to keep me?" Daisy asked the words, although they tasted bitter on her tongue.

"No, not at all. I tried to keep it from my parents as long as I could. They finally realized something was going on when summer came and I refused to swim. They were furious. My mother called me many names but my father, he didn't say a single word. He didn't speak to me for an entire month." Rowena turned to the photos on the side table and Daisy followed her gaze to a photo of an elderly couple… her grandparents.

"When he finally did talk to me, I'd just come around to accepting that I needed to live with the choices I made. Which meant having you and raising you. I knew it would be hard, especially with my father hating me, but I was willing to do it. To give you the life you deserved. It wasn't your fault I was reckless." She turned to Daisy and continued to explain. "My father came home from work one evening and sat me down. He told me he and my mother didn't work their whole lives to watch me throw mine away. They wouldn't stand by and watch me raise a baby in my senior year and wander through college while stringing a baby along."

Daisy swallowed past the pain. She had been seen as a liability, not a blessing. She wasn't sure why, but that hurt her more than not knowing who her mother was at all.

"They agreed to help me through the pregnancy, pay for all the medical expenses, on one condition. I had to give you up. If I didn't, I needed to pack my bags and leave... right there and then."

Ryan shook his head and let out his breath in a huff. "That's rough."

"It was, and I was in no position to argue or to beg. I'd made a mistake," Rowena said, squaring her shoulders. "So I agreed to give you up. They took you from me an hour after you were born. That's all we had together, one hour. The nurse said you'd go into a foster home until they found you a family. I was so afraid you didn't find one." Rowena brushed away a tear that slipped over her cheek.

"I found one," Daisy said, refusing to feel like as if it was her fault that Rowena had to go through that. She wanted to sympathize but she couldn't help but feel as if she was the one drawing the short end of the stick.

"A wunderbaar one. My mamm, Lydia, is the kindest, most affectionate mother I could've asked for. And my daed, Noah—he was the greatest father and farmer."

"That's good, I'm glad to hear that," Rowena smiled, pleased. "I often thought of you over the years."

"I only learned I was adopted six months ago," Daisy returned. "I struggled with it at first, but now I know it was for the best. I'm glad I got to meet you."

"Is that your family?" Ryan asked, pointing to the photos.

Rowena's smiled softened with affection. "Yes, that's Mike and our children. Lisa, Edward, and Jason."

"Do they know about me?" Daisy asked in a small voice. It felt strange to look at photos and to know that those were her blood relatives. Her half brothers and sisters. And yet she felt no connection to them at all.

Not like she felt with Celia and Lucas.

"No," Rowena said quickly, her features hardening. "I never told Mike—he wouldn't understand. I'm sure you can understand that?"

It felt as if Daisy had just been slapped. She hadn't expected her mother to make it blatantly clear that she was a secret.

A dirty little secret that she had tucked away in her past, a past she never revisited. She nodded, trying to ignore the burn in her eyes. She wouldn't cry, not in front of Rowena.

"Like I said, I'm so glad to have met you. To know you were loved and happy." Rowena stood up, making it clear their reunion was over. "I'm going to have to ask you to go now. Lisa will be home any time now. In fact, when you knocked, I thought it was her."

Ryan stood up and moved towards Daisy. He rested a hand on her shoulder, offering her his quiet support. "Yeah, we've got to get going anyhow."

Daisy stood up, feeling her knees quiver slightly beneath her weight. She was stunned wordless by how easy it was for Rowena to turn her back on her a second time.

It felt hollow and cold and nothing like Daisy had imagined it would feel when she finally met her birth mother at all. "Goodbye, Rowena."

She made a point of using Rowena's name, because she wasn't worth the phrase mother.

Only Lydia Eymann would have that privilege in Daisy's life.

Chapter 17
The Familye
That Chose You

Ryan could feel Daisy's hand shake in his as he walked her to the car. He knew she was trying her best to be strong, to not show Rowena how heartbroken she was.

He opened the door for her and waited until she had climbed in before he walked around the car. From the door, Rowena waved to them as if they were strangers that had stopped at the wrong house.

"You take care now," Rowena called out.

Ryan didn't bother answering her, or even waving goodbye.

He couldn't believe the woman's gall. To invite Daisy in, only to tell her she'd been a mistake, one that she'd put in her past. That Daisy had been an inconvenience, that she had made someone else's problem.

She hadn't put it in so many words, but if she had really cared, she would've asked more about Daisy's life. About Daisy's childhood and her family.

But she hardly asked Daisy anything at all. She didn't even mention the fact that Daisy was Amish or asked where she had come from.

It was as if Rowena had simply been appeased by seeing her and as soon as she did, she wanted to be rid of her.

Anything to stop her perfect family from learning about her tainted past.

Ryan started the car and drove a couple of blocks before he pulled over at a park. He climbed out and walked around the car to open Daisy's door.

Ever since she had climbed into the car, she hadn't said a single word. It was as if she was holding back a torrent of emotions that could explode at any moment.

"Come, let's take a walk in the park. We can go sit by the pond?" Ryan suggested.

Daisy climbed out wordlessly. He took her hand and led her to the pond.

She was still shaking from either shock, anger, or disappointment; perhaps a mixture of all of those.

They sat down on a bench, and Daisy stared at the water.

Ryan held her hand, wishing he could do more for her than just be there. "If you want to talk…"

Daisy turned to him. "Nee, I'm done talking about her. I just wasted three days of my life to find her. Three days, only to learn that she was ashamed of me. She didn't even care about my family or where I lived. She didn't even ask me if I wanted to see her again. She just wanted to get rid of me, again." Daisy's voice held so much anger that Ryan was about to suggest a dip in the pond to help her cool off, when suddenly the dam that held back her tears broke.

She cried big fat tears, her shoulders shaking as she let the emotion out. Ryan pulled her close and held her, feeling his own heart break on her behalf.

Ryan didn't know how long she cried; he didn't care. He was just grateful that he was there beside her.

When she finally stopped, she shook her head and smiled at him with disappointment in her eyes. "Now I know."

Ryan nodded. "Now you know. And the best part is, you still have a family that loves you and wants you to be part of their lives. Your proper family."

Daisy nodded and let out a sigh. "They don't even know where I am."

"Then why don't we change that?" Ryan pulled out his phone and handed it to her. "Do you know the number…. Wait, do you have phones?"

Daisy chuckled and shook her head. "There are a few phone shanties in the community. One isn't too far from my haus."

Ryan watched as she dialed a number and waited while the phone rang. When someone answered, Daisy's accent thickened. "Hullo. It's Daisy Eymann. Could you please fetch Celia?"

"Denke," Daisy said when the other person replied.

Ryan realized that now that she had met Rowena, their time together was ending, but he wouldn't think of that yet.

"Hullo, Celia, it's me. Daisy," Daisy said, smiling into the phone when she heard her sister's voice on the other end of the line.

"Nee, I haven't run away. I just needed to… it doesn't matter. How is Mamm, Lucas, and his frau?" Daisy asked.

Ryan patiently waited while Daisy spoke to her sister about where she was and when she planned on returning home. When she ended the call, she turned to him with a grateful smile. "It might not be Gott's plan for me to have Rowena in my life, but he sure planned on blessing me with the best familye ever. Celia was so happy to hear from me."

"I'm sure they were very concerned?" Ryan asked.

Daisy nodded. "Jah, they were. I told her I'd be home late tomorrow afternoon. I thought it would be best if we slept in the motel tonight and then leave for Harrisburg early tomorrow morning? There is a bus late afternoon to Mill Creek.

Ryan shook his head, already wondering how he was going to say goodbye. "I'll take you to Mill Creek. It's the least I can do."

"Ryan, you've already wasted enough of your time," Daisy insisted.

Ryan shook his head and held her gaze, hoping she understood how he felt. "I haven't wasted a single minute."

Daisy's smile broadened as a light flush colored her cheeks. Ryan knew she had understood.

"Then the least I can do is offer to buy you dinner," Daisy said, standing up. "How do you feel about pizza?"

Ryan laughed as he joined Daisy on the walk to the car. "I have only good feelings about pizza."

Chapter 18
Pizza & Promises

The cheese was still sizzling on the pizza when the waiter set it down on their table. Daisy's mouth watered at the scent of pepperoni, cheese, and garlic. "This is enough to feed a family of five."

Ryan chuckled as he helped himself to a piece. "Or just a hungry cab driver and his friend."

Daisy smiled as she helped herself to a piece. For a moment she felt self-conscious about eating with her hands, but a quick glance around the restaurant assured her everyone else was doing it as well.

"I'm your friend?" Daisy asked with a hopeful smile.

Ryan shrugged. "Of course you are. Don't you consider me to be a friend after the last couple of days?"

Daisy thought for a moment and realized that a friend wasn't the label she would've categorized Ryan in. The words soulmate and partner came to mind.

She quickly pushed the words aside, convincing herself that it was simply the emotional upheaval of today that made her think that she and Ryan could be more.

He was Englisch, and that would not change.

"Jah, I consider you to be a friend," she finally agreed.

"This isn't the best pizza I've had, but it comes close. One day, I'll take you to a spot in Harrisburg. Italian owners. No one makes pizza like them. The crust is thin and crispy and they add just the right amount of cheese and garlic to make your mouth sing with joy." Ryan grabbed another piece.

Daisy didn't comment. The last thing she wanted to do was to spoil the evening by reminding Ryan that she wouldn't be going back to Harrisburg in the future.

If this trip had taught her anything, it was that she belonged in Mill Creek. She missed the peace and quiet, her familye, and strangely enough, she missed the predictability of her life in the Amish community.

Although she'd had quite the adventure over the last few days, the hustle and bustle of the Englisch world wasn't for her.

She just wished Ryan could go back to Mill Creek with her.

When she looked up, she noticed Ryan watching her with a concerned look. "Are you all right after today?" He let out a quiet sigh. "If I'd known how Rowena was going to treat you, I would've never insisted we go on to Rowena number three. I should've stopped when you hesitated."

Daisy shook her head. "Nee, it wasn't your fault. I wanted to find her; I just didn't know what I would find. I think in my mind I envisioned a reunion where she embraced me as the daughter I am, and insisted on keeping touch. I just didn't expect to be turned away, as if we had no connection at all. Either way, now I know. Knowing is better than not knowing at all."

"At least you have your family waiting for you back home," Ryan said with a consoling tone.

Daisy's mouth curved into a smile. "Jah, at least I have them. I never really realized how lucky I was to have them until today. To be loved and accepted regardless of being adopted – I don't think every adopted child was as lucky as I was. I'll be forever grateful to Lydia and Noah for that. I can even forgive them now for not telling me. It's easy to understand now that they were just protecting me."

"That's what good parents do," Ryan said with a sad smile.

"I'm sorry your daed didn't stay to protect you after your mamm died. Do you have any other familye? Aunts, uncles, cousins?" Daisy asked hopefully. Perhaps she could encourage him to get in contact with his other family.

"Nope," Ryan shrugged, reaching for a third slice. "Just me, myself, and I. Although, if I'm honest, the car has become like family." He winked at her before taking a bite of his pizza.

Daisy nodded. "It's like our horses become familye, I guess."

"What's it like? Being Amish?" Ryan asked between bites.

Daisy thought for a moment, wondering how she could describe her life to someone from the outside. "It's predictable."

Daisy chuckled softly before she met Ryan's gaze. "It's peaceful to start with. There's no noise like here in the city. In the mornings, I can hear the farm wake up. I can hear the birds, the neighbors' cows lowing in the distance, the chickens, and of course, the rooster. You can smell the rain before it falls and on a hot day you can smell the trees that grow on the hill."

"It sounds… magical," Ryan said, listening attentively, the pizza forgotten.

"There's a lot of work. We don't have any electricity or technology to interfere with how we do things. We each have chores each morning and each evening. Then there's Mamm to look after. She has her gut days and her not so gut days, but we don't mind. She looked after us for many years when we were little. Now it's our turn," Daisy said, smiling affectionately at the memory of her mother.

"So, you all work on the farm?" Ryan asked, intrigued.

Daisy shook her head. "Nee, just Lucas works on the farm. I'm a teacher's assistant at school. My schweschder Celia mostly takes care of Mamm and takes care of the housekeeping. Lucas's frau works at social services in town as a volunteer three days a week."

"Sound like a busy life," Ryan commented.

"It is. But on Sundays we rest. We have church every second Sunday and on the Sundays in between, we either visit friends or spend the day with each other. We usually cook an enormous meal and after lunch we rest. In summer, Celia and I go swimming in the creek."

"Don't you get bored? You don't have television to watch to kill time or go out to see new things…" Ryan asked hesitantly.

Daisy realized he was curious, but didn't want to offend her.

"Nee, we don't get bored. There's always something to do and if we want to *kill time*, there is always the bible. You can never learn enough from Gott's word," Daisy smiled. "Of course, we have activities we also enjoy. Celia is part of a quilting group; I also do some quilting. We have our prayer groups, there is the jamming bees. There's always something to do if you don't want to be bored."

"And your… faith? How does that work? Do you have to like pray several times a day or you're chased away?"

Daisy couldn't help but laugh. "I don't know what you've heard, but it was wrong. Our faith is part of who we are, not a threat or a punishment. The only reasons for being shunned are committing a crime that violates Gott's word, infidelity, and consorting with Englischers on an intimate level."

"That isn't so bad," Ryan shrugged.

"Exactly, like I said it's not like we're bound by a blood oath, Ryan, we simply choose to live in a way that honors our faith, respects family and community, and denounces outside influences which will detract from our faith," Daisy explained.

"I wish I had faith like yours. It seems pretty amazing to see how you practice it naturally. It's so much a part of you I don't think you even realize it," Ryan said, meeting her gaze.

Daisy felt her heart skip a beat. Ryan was looking at her in a way that made her feel as if she was much more than just a friend. "It's who I am."

Ryan kept holding her gaze as he reached across the table and took her hand in his. "I like who you are. You're the most amazing woman I've ever met."

Daisy knew the feelings that were making her heart swell had more to do with love than friendship, but she was helpless to break the spell.

She'd never looked at a man and felt her heart blossom with hopes of a future. "You're the kindest man I've ever met."

"It's a shame we found your birth mother. I would've enjoyed spending a few more days with you."

Daisy nodded, knowing she felt the same.

"Would you like anything else?" the waitress interrupted them. Daisy snatched her hand away and quickly looked at the pizza to avoid Ryan seeing her flushed cheeks.

"Just the check," Ryan responded.

Daisy reached into her purse for the money when Ryan stopped her. "This is on me."

"But I said I owe you dinner. If it wasn't for me, you wouldn't even have been in Millersburg," Daisy argued.

Ryan shook his head and placed his hand on her arm to stop her from taking out her money. "Let me treat you to dinner. It's the least I can do after everything I've learned from you."

Daisy was helpless to argue. The way he looked at her robbed her of speech. She nodded and put her purse away.

While Ryan settled the bill, Daisy was both grateful and sad that their journey would end tomorrow. She was grateful because she was afraid that if she spent more time with Ryan, she might forget the rules that prohibited her from falling in love with him.

At the same time, she was sad, because she wasn't sure she'd ever meet another man as wonderful as him.

Chapter 19
Journey's End

They left for Mill Creek just before dawn.

Although Daisy said nothing, Ryan could detect after their dinner last night that she was eager to get home. They rode in silence for most of the way, only stopping in Harrisburg for gas and something to eat.

Ryan had never been to Lancaster County before and enjoyed the drive from Harrisburg to Mill Creek. He watched the landscape change from city buildings and traffic into farmlands and small communities.

Just like Daisy had explained to him, it was a different world, a different life.

They talked about inconsequential things when they talked. Like commenting on the height of a tree, or a crop of corn, or even just pointing out landmarks to each other.

The radio quietly played in the background, as if to drown out the silences in between. Silences laden with unspoken words.

There was so much Ryan wanted to say to her, so much that he couldn't.

If it hadn't been for her faith and her commitment to the Amish way of life, Ryan would have told her he'd like to spend more time with her.

He would've asked her on a date and hoped that one date would lead to more.

For the first time since losing his parents, the hollowness in his chest had been filled. Filled with feelings of affection, acceptance, and love.

Ryan knew it was ridiculous to think of love after only knowing Daisy for a few days, but it didn't feel ridiculous to him.

For him, it felt like he had found the missing piece of his heart and now he was going to leave it somewhere where he wasn't welcome.

He glanced at Daisy and felt his heart clench in his chest. *How was he going to say goodbye?*

"As soon as you're through town, you turn left onto the dirt road at the large red barn on your left," Daisy explained as they drove through the town of Mill Creek.

To Ryan, it looked like the postcard image of a small town. There were no franchise stores, only owner-owned stores with original names like Bob's Hardware. He followed the road and turned left at the big red barn. "Do I just carry on straight?" Ryan asked as they drove into farmlands. White houses and red barns dotted the landscape even as crop fields stood tall in between.

"Jah, up there you'll see an old windmill. You can turn right there."

Ryan smiled at her directions. His GPS showed a road, but no road names. This was an area completely unchartered by English technology.

"There's the school," Daisy pointed to a small building with black shutters and a small play area.

"It looks nice," Ryan said, imagining how much fun it would be to swing on the swing that hung from an old tree.

"It is," Daisy agreed.

Ryan turned and slowed the car even more as a buggy came from the other direction. The man wore a black suit and a straw wide brim hat. He tipped the hat as he drove past Ryan. It was as if he'd just travelled into a different century.

When he finally turned into a yard, he was surprised by how neat it was. Regardless of there being a chicken coop and outbuildings, including a barn and stables, there wasn't a single item out of place.

Even the buggy seemed to have its spot underneath a shade net beside the barn.

"This is it, my haus," Daisy said with excitement brimming in her eyes. It was a little after lunch time and Ryan couldn't help but feel deflated he would be back in the city before nightfall.

"Denke, kumm meet my familye," Daisy said happily before she climbed out of the car.

Ryan was barely out of the car when he saw a woman running from the house towards Daisy. She wore the same dress and white prayer kapp as Daisy.

"Daisy! You're home! Lucas! Kumm see!"

"Celia!" Daisy cried out and met her halfway. They embraced each other for a moment before a tall man with dark hair came rushing towards them. He embraced both women before he stood back and took a good look at Daisy.

"Denke Gott, I was so worried about you. Don't you ever frighten us like that again." His voice was thick with emotion.

Ryan reasoned that to be Daisy's brother, Lucas. It was clear how much the three siblings cared for each other, regardless of being adopted.

Another woman stepped onto the porch, keeping her distance for the moment, but looking just as pleased by Daisy's return.

"Kumm, I'd like you to meet Ryan Ascot," Daisy said, leading her brother and sister towards Ryan. "Ryan was my cab driver in Harrisburg and went out of his way to take me to Millersburg and bring me all the way back home," Daisy explained.

Ryan could feel Lucas's eyes on him, trying to assess whether he should be grateful to Ryan or dislike him.

Once the introductions were made and Daisy had collected her luggage, Ryan knew it was time for him to leave.

"I better get going. It's still a long drive back to Harrisburg. It was nice to meet all of you," Ryan said, taking a step towards his car. His gaze met Daisy's, and he felt his heart break into a million pieces.

"Why don't you stay for dinner? You brought Daisy home and kept her safe. It's the least we can do," Lucas offered.

"Celia, you can make chicken fried steak. I told Ryan all about how wunderbaar your steak is," Daisy suggested excitedly.

Ryan wasn't sure if he should accept or decline. He didn't want to get Daisy into trouble.

"Then it's settled. You'll stay for chicken-fried steak. We can make up a bed for you for the night, then you can leave in the morning," Lucas said with the authority of the man of the house.

"Kumm, meet my mamm," Daisy said, inviting him inside before Ryan could accept or decline.

"I'll go get started on dinner," Celia announced, heading up to the house.

Ryan wasn't sure what to expect from having dinner with an Amish family, but he didn't expect to feel welcomed and treated as if he were an honored guest.

He met Lydia, and could quickly see that although she was suffering from Alzheimer's, she had been a kind and caring mother.

Unlike Rowena.

After dinner, Lucas's wife excused herself to help Lydia to bed, leaving the siblings alone for the first time, with only Ryan joining them.

"Did you find her?" Celia asked hesitantly.

Ryan saw Lucas clench his jaw. Clearly, Lucas hadn't been fond of the thought of Daisy looking for her mother.

Ryan sat quietly and listened as Daisy told them about what had happened over the last few days. When she reached the part about Rowena asking her to leave, he wanted to reach out to her and offer her support. But he couldn't, not with her family sitting there to judge.

Celia consoled her with a hug and a few kind words. Lucas surprised Ryan by getting up and laying a hand on Daisy's shoulder before he spoke. "This is the only familye that matters. This is the familye Gott chose for us. Here you are loved, wanted, and cherished. Always remember that."

Ryan's throat clogged with emotion at hearing such a big and masculine man say such kind words to his sister. He'd thought that Daisy was special, but Ryan now realized her family was just as special.

He secretly wished that he too could be part of such a special family.

Lucas and his wife retired for the evening after that. Celia talked to Daisy a little more about her mother and how she had been doing while Daisy was away before she also retired for the evening. Knowing that was his cue to go to bed, Ryan stood up and thanked them for a wonderful evening.

Celia and Daisy shared a look before Celia left them alone.

Daisy moved towards him with a warm smile. "Denke for staying. My familye likes you very much."

Ryan smiled. "They're a special family. Just like you."

Daisy reached for his hand and squeezed it briefly before she let it go. "I hope you sleep well, Ryan."

"You too, Daisy."

Ryan climbed into bed a few minutes later, but knew that sleep wouldn't come. He didn't want to miss a single minute of spending time in this wonderful community with this special family.

He already knew that he would cherish the memories of this evening for the rest of his life.

Chapter 20
No Remedy for
a Broken Heart

Saying goodbye to Ryan had to be the hardest thing Daisy had ever had to do. She could only compare it to standing beside her father's grave and knowing she'd never see him again.

That was how she felt in the days after Ryan returned to Harrisburg.

School was still out, so she didn't even have the luxury of having the children to distract her for a few hours a day. Instead, she found chores to do around the house, deep-cleaned the bedrooms, and washed the windows to occupy her hands when she couldn't occupy her mind.

All she kept thinking was that she would never hear his laughter again.

She would never have him look at her with affection and kindness.

Ryan would never hold her hand again or tell her how special she was.

It was a strange emptiness, one that began in a small part of her heart and as the hours passed, grew a little bigger each day.

The worst part was that she couldn't even confide in someone to tell them of her heartbreak.

As far as her family was concerned, they thought she was still trying to process her meeting with Rowena. But Daisy had dealt with that on the drive back home. She had put Rowena and their meeting in a place in her mind she chose to never visit again.

Instead, she focused on being grateful for her family and knowing that here she was accepted.

Here was where she belonged.

But neither Lucas, Celia, or Sarah would understand that she was quiet and withdrawn because of the Englischer that had returned to his home in the city.

Where he belonged.

After collecting the laundry from the line one afternoon, Daisy offered to spend time with her mother so Celia could go to her quilting group. Sarah was in town at the soup kitchen and Lucas was working in the fields.

Her mother sat quietly, looking out the window. Daisy joined her, enjoying the silence.

After a while, her mother turned to her with a questioning look. "I've seen the look in your eyes for a few days now," her mother reached for her hand and smiled as if she understood how Daisy felt.

"It's nothing, I just have a lot on my mind," Daisy quickly dismissed her mother's concern.

"A woman only has that look when she has love on her mind," Lydia said with a smile. Her eyes were clear and her mind was lucid, as if her disease had never affected her at all.

Daisy cherished these moments, wishing her mother would stay with her and not fade away again.

"It doesn't matter, Mamm, it's not meant to be," Daisy admitted finally, feeling her heart break all over again.

"How would you know? Have you read Genesis?" Lydia asked with a cocked brow. *"Genesis 2:18 The Lord Gott says, it is not good for the man to be alone. I will make a suitable partner for him."*

Daisy chuckled. "And what about the woman? Will he make a suitable partner for her as well?"

"Of course he has. He made one just for you," Lydia assured her.

"It can't work, Mamm, it can't ever work," Daisy admitted, her voice cracking with emotion.

Lydia squeezed her hand and smiled confidently into her daughter's sad eyes. "Where there is Gott, there is a way. Where there is love, there is hope. And where there are obstacles, there are solutions. You only have to pray."

Daisy smiled, although she knew her mother didn't understand. How could she and Ryan ever overcome the obstacles in their way? She couldn't abandon her faith, her community, or her family.

And Ryan would never abandon the Englisch life he was accustomed to.

But she couldn't tell her mother that. She didn't want to disappoint her mother by telling her she had fallen in love with an Englischer. It would break her mother's heart.

Instead, Daisy nodded. "Then I'll pray."

"Gut," Lydia nodded. "Prayer is the answer to everything. I too, will pray that your obstacles fade away and that the road is cleared for your heart to find your suitable partner."

Daisy's eyes burned with emotion, but she bit back the tears.

If only prayer could bring her a miracle.

Chapter 21
Love Is Patient &
Love Is Protective

Ryan rubbed his palms against his thighs, hoping the fabric of his jeans would absorb the clamminess. He couldn't remember ever being this nervous before.

His heart was beating in his chest to a loud beat, so loud that he could hear the blood rushing in his ears.

The sounds of the coffee shop faded away as his anxiety made him aware of every second that ticked by.

He wasn't sure if he had come all the way for nothing, and if he did that meant it was time for him to put his feelings for Daisy, along with the memories of the few days they had spent together, behind him.

When he had left Mill Creek two weeks ago, he had been certain that he would never return, or see Daisy again. But with every day that passed, with every passenger he picked up in the city, Ryan felt more and more out of place.

He began seeing Harrisburg through Daisy's eyes and instead of just missing her; he missed the life she had described to him.

A life he had never experienced before and now longed for.

He had researched on the internet for hours on end about how it would work if he wanted to join an Amish congregation, and the more he learned, the more he realized that was what he wanted to do.

Ever since he had lost his parents he had felt out of place, unwanted, and as if he were a piece of driftwood floating with the current, with no control over his future.

This was the first time Ryan knew what he wanted from his future since before his mother had become ill.

The feeling was exciting, but at the same time it was terrifying. What if, just like the last time he had plans for his future, they were ruined before he could pursue them?

Today his fate lie in the hands of one man. A man he'd only met once before.

Lucas Eymann.

Ryan knew he could approach the bishop of the congregation directly and ask him for permission to join the community and to begin his proving period, but Ryan also understood that if he wanted a future with Daisy that wasn't the right way to go about it.

If he wanted a future with Daisy, he needed Lucas's blessing before he even considered talking to the bishop.

He still had the phone shanty's number in his call history and had used it to contact Lucas. Lucas had been just as surprised to hear from Ryan as Ryan was that he had made the call.

He had asked Lucas to meet him here today, hoping that he could convince Lucas of his true intentions and perhaps earn his blessing to join the congregation.

The bells jingled on the door, and Ryan turned to see Lucas enter the coffee shop. His heart raced nervously in his chest as he stood up to greet Lucas with a handshake. Lucas's smile was hesitant as he joined Ryan. "Ryan, hullo."

"Hi Lucas, thanks for meeting me," Ryan said, sitting down. "I wasn't sure if you'd come or not."

"If I give my word, I honor it. What can I do for you, you mentioned it was a matter best discussed in person?" Lucas asked, not wasting time before getting to the point.

Ryan debated for a moment if he should start with his feelings for Daisy or his yearning to lead their way of life. He drew in a deep breath and met Lucas's gaze. "I'm not sure how to say this, or even if you'll understand, but… I'd like to join your congregation. Ever since meeting Daisy and spending an evening in your home, I've come to understand what was missing from my life. I never understood it until then. I would like nothing more than to lead a life doing honest work. A life where my faith and my community come first. I've been drifting for years, not knowing what to do or where I wanted to be, and now for the first time I feel as if I've been called by God. I've… I've often neglected my religion in the past, but I realize now that it's the modern way of life that detracts and distracts you. I want that to end," Ryan finished, almost breathless.

He had talked so fast, hoping to get everything out before he lost his courage, that he could only hope that Lucas had followed.

Lucas frowned and tilted his head with a curious look. "You want to leave all the luxuries, technologies, and comforts of an Englisch life behind to join our congregation?

That isn't an easy decision to make. It's not one you can turn back from?"

Ryan nodded. "I realize that. I have no intention of turning my back on my community once I'm baptized."

Lucas's eyes widened before he let out a sigh. "That's all gut and well, but if you want to join the congregation, you'll have to talk to our bishop. There would be a proving period. You'll need a host familye where you can live until you're baptized–you'll need to distance yourself from all your Englisch belongings…"

"I know. But before I go to see the bishop, I wanted to talk to you first. I know it isn't acceptable for me to have any feelings towards your sister, as an Englischer, an outsider—" Ryan stopped when Lucas interrupted.

"Daisy? You only spent three days with her… how could you…?" Lucas asked, baffled.

"Because I know. Daisy is the most wonderful person I've ever met. She reminded me how important family is. The way she spoke of her life here, of her family. The way she exercises her faith in any situation and always carries hope for a good outcome. It's not acceptable for me to say that I've fallen in love with her, especially because I'm still Englisch. But I want to ask for your blessing, that when I'm baptized, after I pass my proving period, that I can court Daisy. Hopefully, if she feels the same way, I can spend the rest of my life trying to bring her the happiness she brought me." Ryan let out a sigh. "I know you think that I'm crazy, that I'm probably just wasting your time and that I'll break her heart, but I can promise you I'm not and I won't."

"How do I know I can take your word for it?" Lucas asked, the protective look in his eyes making it clear he doubted Ryan's intentions.

"Because love is patient and kind and it doesn't bring harm. That is what I feel for Daisy. I won't jeopardize her position in the community until I know I can make her a good Amish husband, but until then I hope I can get to know her better, with your blessing, of course. I'm spending a few days in Mill Creek to get everything in order. As soon as you give me your blessing, I'd like to see the bishop."

Lucas stood up, shook his head and met Ryan's gaze head on. "Personally, I think that you're lost and hoping my baby schweschder can redeem you. She's got enough on her plate as it is. I'm grateful for the help you gave her in the city, but I cannot condone this. I will not. Daisy deserves more than an Englischer trying to be who he isn't just to win her favor. Enjoy your time in Mill Creek. Goodbye Ryan."

Ryan had never felt more crushed than watching Lucas leave the coffee shop. He'd thought Lucas might be firm, threaten him even if he hurt Daisy.

He didn't expect Lucas to rebuff him and walk out on him without bothering to even try to understand how Ryan felt.

He couldn't help but wish he'd contacted Daisy instead. Perhaps if she'd spoken to her brother on his behalf, things might have been different.

But it was too late now for what if's.

Chapter 22
Heart & Mind at War

"Daisy, will you mind helping Mamm to bed?" Lucas asked when they had finished dinner.

Sarah frowned at him curiously, as she had been doing it most nights ever since their wedding. Even Daisy looked surprised by the request. "Of course."

Lucas waited until he heard Daisy close her mother's bedroom door before he met Celia and Sarah's questioning looks with a resigned look of his own. "I need to talk to both of you."

"Has something happened?" Celia asked, joining Lucas and Sarah at the table after putting away the last dish.

"Nee, I mean jah. It's hard to explain." Lucas let out a heavy sigh. "I met with Ryan today."

"The cab driver that brought Daisy home?" Sarah asked, surprised.

"Jah." Lucas nodded. He glanced at Celia and Sarah before he relayed to them the conversation he had had with Ryan earlier that day. Ever since he had returned from town, he had been wondering if he had done the right thing.

He didn't want Daisy's reputation to be harmed or her position in the community to be jeopardized by an

Englischer, but at the same time, he didn't want to be the one determining her future without her knowledge.

Isn't that what their parents had done their whole lives by not telling them about their adoptions?

When he was finished, he shook his head and shrugged. "In my mind I know I did the right thing—an Englischer has no place here."

"But in your heart?" Sarah asked carefully.

"In my heart I fear Daisy feels the same way about him and that she'll never forgive me if she learns I turned him away," Lucas admitted with a heavy heart.

Celia, who hadn't said a word the entire time, finally spoke up. "Do you think he wants to join our community just because he hopes to court Daisy, or do you think he actually wants to pursue a life the Amish way?"

"That's the thing. He seemed sincere when he spoke of joining the congregation. I truly believe that he honestly wants to step away from the Englisch world and become Amish, but how I can know that for sure, when he admits he has feelings for Daisy?"

"Daisy has been very off lately. I thought it was because of what happened to her birth mother, but now that you mention this… I think she misses him as well," Sarah added with a quiet sigh of her own.

"I don't want her to get hurt, Sarah. When my daed passed it fell to me to protect this familye. If I don't look out for her, who will?" Lucas demanded quietly.

"Gott will," Celia answered. "Lucas, if Ryan's intentions weren't pure or well thought through, he would've gone over your head directly to the bishop. He would've arrived here one day to announce he was now part of the community and the next thing we knew he would've been engaged to our Daisy. He thought it well to see you first. To ask for your permission. It sounds to me as if he let you in on his deepest thoughts and desires for the future. Do you really think he would've done that if he didn't really have feelings for Daisy, or respect our way of living?"

Lucas couldn't help but admit that Celia was right. "So I made a mistake?"

"Nee, you acted in haste. There is a difference," Sarah consoled her husband.

"See him tomorrow. You said he's staying in town for a few days… Tell him you approve. And then you offer him the hayloft for his proving period. What better way to see if his intentions are true to have him live with us during his proving period? You could use the help on the farm, especially with harvest season coming up, and you can teach him how to be the Amish husband Daisy deserves. That way, when the time comes for him to be baptized into the community, you will know his character," Celia explained.

Sarah nodded. "She's right Lucas. If you're concerned, what better way to look out for Daisy than to take Ryan under your wing, so to speak?"

"And if she doesn't feel the same way?" Lucas asked, fearing for his sister's heart.

"Then she won't allow him to court her, as simple as that. But if she does, Lucas, he could be her future," Celia said with a hopeful smile. "Mamm always said love finds a way."

Lucas nodded, realizing that he could protect his sisters, but at the end of the day he couldn't protect them from everything and everyone. "I'll think about it."

"Gut. But I think you already know what you need to do," Celia said firmly as she stood up from the table. "Perhaps our Daisy might even smile again before school starts in a couple of weeks."

Chapter 23
New Beginnings

"How was your first day back at school?" Sarah asked, just as Daisy stepped through the door.

She set down her basket filled with books, stationery, and activities and met Sarah's question with a smile. "Wunderbaar. I didn't realize how much I missed the kinner. They had so many stories about their holiday, we could barely teach a lesson today."

"I'm sure they missed you as well," Celia said from her seat in the living room, where she was working on a quilt.

It was just after three o'clock and Daisy felt exhausted after her first day back at school. Besides the walk to the schoolhouse and back, she had been on her feet most of the day.

Around the children it was as if she fed off their endless energy, but now that she had arrived home, she wanted nothing more than a cup of tea and some quiet.

"How was Mamm's day?" Daisy asked her mother as she kneeled before her.

"Very gut," Lydia smiled and turned to look out the window again.

"It was a quiet day; she's been tired for most of the day," Celia explained. "I don't think she slept well last night."

"Who could?" Daisy asked. "The wind knocked that branch against the house all night. We really should ask Lucas to cut it off."

"Already did," Sarah said with a smile before she turned to Celia. "If you want me to learn how to quilt, I'm going to need a quilting basket of my own."

Sarah glanced down at the rounds of cotton at her feet and shook her head. "Your things are so neat, and all kept together in one place."

Celia smiled at her sister-in-law. "I know just what you need. Daisy, do you remember my first quilting basket? The small one with the divisions where I used to keep my cottons?"

Daisy laughed. "Jah, you carried it around everywhere."

"Until I got this one. Would you mind fetching it from the hayloft for Sarah?" Celia asked before she carefully threaded a piece of cotton through the quilt she was working on.

Daisy wanted to let out a sigh and remind her sister that she had been running after children all day, but she resisted. After all, her sister had done all the household chores and cared for her mother all day. "Sure."

Daisy headed across the yard to the hayloft. Lucas was working in the fields, not too far from the house, and waved to her. Daisy waved back before she walked into the barn. The scent of hay, horses, and feed met her as she stepped inside.

She glanced at the ladder to the hayloft and let out a quiet sigh. Did Celia know how uncomfortable it was to climb the ladder with a dress?

Carefully, she climbed the ladder, rung for rung. Taking her time with each step. The hayloft had been used to store hay by previous generations, but for her family it had always been a storage space.

As soon as Daisy reached the top, she realized they had moved things around. She hadn't been in the hayloft for years, but she could remember there hadn't been a wall separating one part from the other.

Curious, she moved towards the divider that hadn't been there before when she heard footsteps on the other side.

Her heart jumped into her throat, realizing she wasn't alone. "Hullo?"

Daisy had heard of squatters, but she imagined no one would want to squat in a hayloft, especially not theirs.

She carefully took another step forward and caught sight of a man standing with his back to her. "Hullo?" Daisy repeated a little louder.

The man turned around and Daisy's heart all but stopped. It must be the lack of sleep or symptoms of a broken heart, she reasoned, as she imagined herself it was Ryan standing there.

"Hi Daisy," he said with a hesitant smile.

Daisy's eyes widened with surprise. "Ryan, is it really you?"

Ryan shrugged and pulled at the lapels of his jacket. "The clothes might be different and I no longer have a car, but it's me."

Realizing she wasn't imagining things, Daisy took another step forward. "But how, why..."

Ryan laughed. "It's a long story."

Daisy listened as Ryan told her everything that had happened since the last time she had seen him. Her heart swelled with joy when she learned he was joining the community, but it swelled even more to know that Lucas had offered him the hayloft to live in during his proving period.

"So you're staying?" Daisy asked, as hope and excitement for her future exploded in her soul.

"I don't intend to ever leave again. And when I'm finally baptized, and I'm the Amish mann you deserve to spend your life with, I'd like to take you on a buggy ride." Ryan chuckled. "I'll probably have to borrow your brother's, but I'm sure he won't mind."

Daisy shook her head as happy tears rolled over her cheeks. "Here I thought I was coming to search for a basket and instead I found you. I thought I'd never see you again."

Ryan reached for her hand and held it as he searched her eyes. "I hope I'll never lose you again."

"Daisy, did you find it?" Lucas called from below.

Daisy laughed. "I found him, denke Lucas."

Lucas's laughter drifted up to her. "Gut, now he can start with his chores. He's been waiting for you all afternoon."

Daisy smiled into Ryan's eyes and knew that no matter what the future held or what the past entailed, she would face anything gladly, knowing that she had Ryan by her side.

Ryan, her family, and, of course, Gott.

*** The End ***

Thank you kindly for choosing to read my book. I sincerely hope you enjoyed it. All of my Amish Romances are wholesome stories suitable for all to enjoy.

If you could be so kind to leave a review on Amazon, I would appreciate it.